On the Road

Laura Muto

To those of you wondering if things could have turned out differently if you had just done a little bit of this or a little bit of that.

Part One

Chapter 1

I HATE TAKE-OFFS. I *despise* them. My leg is bouncing rapidly- all because of a mixture of excitement and nervousness. I'm doing this. *We're* doing this.

We got a phone call from Samantha about two weeks ago, and after plenty of nights of pacing my bedroom and banging my head against the wall, I was able to get onto this plane. We are heading to Hollywood, and I could not be more excited. And scared. I mean, our YouTube channel has taken off; I'm talking about millions on top of millions of views, likes, and comments. Thousands of fans.

My leg bounces again.

"Gia, are you okay?" Luca whispers softly. He places his hand on my leg, trying to calm me down.

Luca and I are... we're great. We are beyond great. If I could go back in time and yell at myself to just admit my feelings sooner, I would.

"Is somebody afraid of flying?" Tony raises his dark, bushy eyebrows at me and drops his head.

"Leave me alone." I dramatically adjust myself so my legs are no longer facing Tony and grab onto my teddy bear. Yes, I took my Groovey bear with me because it reminds me of home and because I've had it since I was a child- I wouldn't want Groovey to miss this opportunity.

Although I'm extremely nervous, I could not be more ecstatic. The fact that someone saw our work, thought we could make it, and offered us a deal still blows my mind. And it all started from a dream. My dream.

The seatbelt light turns on and my leg is back to its bouncing ways. I just simply hate take-offs because of the feeling I get in the pit of my stomach. But it should be a bit better this time because of where we are going.

"Hollywood," I whisper to no one at all, but the boys snap their heads to me instantly. Did I mention that I also hate sitting in the middle seat?

"It's all a bit crazy, isn't it?" Tony responds seriously this time. "To think that once upon a time in a land so far away, we were singing in my basement. We were children not knowing what-"

Nevermind. "Tony," I groan, only giving him encouragement as he continues to stare off into the distance.

He lifts his shoulders up and down. "You knew this was going to happen, Giovanna. It's why we started this in the first place."

But it was still surprising to get that phone call. Despite backing my every move, it was still shocking to me that my family encouraged me to go. They let me say goodbye so I could chase my dreams. I'm already homesick, but I know I'm doing the right thing. I know that I was meant to be on this earth so I can change a little girl's life. I want to be the person little kids look up to.

Luca offers me his hand as soon as the plane starts rolling, and I take it without a second thought. I can tell I'm hurting him because his olive hand turns into a pasty white with how hard I'm squeezing, but he doesn't say a word. He lets me practically break his hand because that's just who he is. Luca is the most caring person I know, and I will do everything in my power to protect him. I will do everything in my power to not break his heart. I just hope he won't break mine.

I let out a huge sigh of relief once we're smoothly flying through the air and the seatbelt light has turned off. I finally let go of Luca's hand and I hear a small grimace escape his lips. "Gia, you weren't joking when you told me you work out every day."

"Every day." I nod my head. I'm going to miss my home gym, I'm going to miss dance class and my friends, but I'm sure I'll be able to find something to do in Hollywood. It is Hollywood, after all.

I cling to my teddy bear, a reminder that everything is still fine back home. I open my mouth to ask Tony to get up so I can use the washroom, but I clamp it shut once I see his eyes are closed and he's snoring. He is always snoring. Always. Seriously, he can fall asleep anywhere at any given time; I'm jealous.

Luca wraps his arm around me and whispers into my ear as he pulls me closer. "Imagine how nice it is to fall asleep without needing melatonin."

I nod at him with big eyes. "I can't believe you got me addicted to that crap."

He bites his lip and I see a thought pass through his eyes, but he doesn't say what's on his mind. "There could be worse things."

A sudden awkward tension comes between us, building higher and higher until I feel like I'm about to drown in a pool of discomfort. "Right."

He knows.

There's no way he knows.

This battle of voices in my head goes through me every night. I actually can't fall asleep without melatonin now because I keep thinking about our first performance as Insieme. I didn't think I was doing anything wrong at the time, and part of me still thinks there was nothing wrong. The problem I have is that I didn't tell the boys. I'm hiding from them. They don't know that I filled my water bottle with alcohol right before we left, and all of me hopes it stays that way.

I feel disgusted with myself because only days before the performance, Tony came out to us, making it clear that we don't keep secrets from each other. We are close enough that we can share anything, but this feels different. I know for a fact that they will judge me, even if they say they aren't mad.

This is what keeps me up at night. I haven't drank a drop of liquor since because I still feel the hangover from drinking for three days in a row. I don't want to feel like that ever again, so I won't touch a bottle again unless there is a party. It just won't happen again; I can't hide it from the boys anymore. I don't want to hide anything from them.

"Gia, I just want you to know that if you ever need to tell me anything, you can come to me," Luca says softly, his voice barely a whisper. "I'm here for you."

He knows.

I run my fingers through his soft wavy hair and look into those puppy dog eyes. "Don't worry about me." *I'm fine.*

He gives me a shy smile. "You know I always worry."

I stretch my neck up until our lips meet. "Everything is going to be alright." I can't tell who I'm trying to convince, myself or Luca.

"As long as you guys stay off of each other for two seconds."

I jump off Luca's chest and swat Tony's arm. "You were snoring literally one minute ago."

He rolls his eyes and drops his ball cap down, hiding the majority of his face. "What can I say? I'm perfect and know everything."

I sink into my seat and groan. This is going to be fun.

Chapter 2

"THIS IS SMALL," Tony complains as soon as we step foot into the hotel.

I heave a heavy sigh and plop onto one of the beds. "We haven't even been here for five minutes and you're already complaining."

"I brought too much stuff for this dinky little thing," he sneers at the tiny dresser. "But it will have to do for now, I guess."

"Unless you have a pile of money burning a whole in the back of your pocket, this is what we got," Luca says, sitting down next to me.

The thing is, our parents were more than supportive of us coming out here, but that doesn't mean we want to take advantage of them. We're paying for this hotel room with our savings because we want to do this on our own, so we have no one to blame if this doesn't work out.

"It's only temporary," Tony continues, opening every drawer and cupboard. "I'm expecting this whole thing to work out so I can buy my dream million dollar home."

"One step at a time," I whisper.

"I'm only joking!" Tony leaps onto the bed where Luca and I are sitting, nearly sending us flying. "Isn't this amazing? We're actually doing this." He squeezes himself in between us and wraps his arms around our shoulders.

Luca flashes a pearly white smile that reaches his eyes. "I'm so excited, and this is only the beginning."

I return his smile with one of my own and lean into Tony's chest. "I already feel like I'm on top of the world."

And I mean it. I've already proved to myself that I can do anything I want to do. I said I wanted to become a singer, and here I am. I proved to myself that I am strong, and that I can be successful. Of course, I have no idea what Insieme is going to look like two weeks from now, but I'm happy with what I already have.

The rest is just gravy.

But I would be lying to you if I said that I didn't want to get more. I want to go on tour and release albums and sell out stadiums; that's what I'm striving for.

"I think it's about time we go for a walk," Luca suggests, eager as always. He doesn't have to tell me twice.

The air is different; I can't explain it. It's more… airy? The air back home seems so dense compared to here, it's a nice change; it's lighter.

Luca grabs my hand and starts humming "Here Comes the Sun"; it's become our song. When I oversleep- which is every single day- he'll wake me up with the song or sing it to me when I'm laying on his chest. I lean my head on his shoulder, swinging our hands back and forth.

I couldn't be happier.

"I could get used to this," I whisper low enough for only Luca to hear.

He plants a gentle kiss on the crown of my forehead. "Me too."

The three of us walk- well, the boys walk, but I'm basically running- in silence for a while, taking in our surroundings. This is fun. It's exciting. It's different. It's new.

I squeeze Luca's hand tighter. "I'm glad we went."

I was getting cold feet as soon as we booked our flight. Should I stay or should I go? My brain told me to stay because everything was good as it was. I was comfortable with my routine, though it seemed like I was repeating the days over and over again. My heart, and others, told me to go. To step into this unknown part of my life.

The unknown doesn't look too bad now, it's actually really pretty out here. I mean, I wouldn't be walking along the Malibu beach if I were back home.

Tony stops suddenly, putting up his hand to motion us to follow suit. He turns his body to the beach and stares with an open mouth. I don't blame him. It looks like the sun is falling into the water; it's beautiful. The sky is no longer vibrant blue, it's a mixture of warm oranges and yellows with hints of pink. I've never seen anything quite like it.

"Luca?" I say softly, but he doesn't hear me because his only focus is on the sunset. "Luca?"

He turns to me, grabbing me by my waist. "Yes, *amore*."

I blush at the name, my cheeks turning as red as the sky. "I think we should come down here every night."

"If that's what you want to do, then we'll do it."

He leans down and gives me a kiss, and I wrap my arms around his neck. We close the space between us until there is none.

Standing here, with my best friends and the sunset, I feel like titanium. Nothing can stop me. Nothing will stop me.

I already have the world.

Chapter 3

I'M EXCITED TO FINALLY put a face to Samantha's voice. I'm expecting a petite woman with a bob cut, but Tony says she's most definitely tall with blonde straight hair. We're about to find out who's right anyways, since the GPS says we're only four minutes away.

Our first day at the Reen's office is going to be a great one, I just know it. I'm so excited to record "I Was Wrong" properly, although I'm thankful for the video Giancarlo took of us at the restaurant. My song is going to be recorded by a professional company and it's going to be a hit.

I know I really shouldn't, but I do anyway. I look at all the comments on our YouTube channel, and a lot of fans are excited to hear our single come out. After our video blew up, we hopped on our channel and told them about our deal. Their congratulations were overwhelming and unexpected. To have complete strangers comment that they're proud of us is a feeling that I don't think we will ever get used to it.

I know that the boys don't look at the comments at all, and they only know about our supporters because I pick and choose what to tell them. Considering that they wanted to delete the video after Sonia's comment, I don't think they would have even moved out here if they saw the other hate comments.

There are those who are our number one supporters, but there are also those who have nothing better to do with their time. They're so judgemental, even though we're doing better than most people.

Constructive criticism is understandable, but these people are straight up assholes. They say we sound off-pitch, unorganized, and just overall bad. They like to direct all their comments to me especially. A lot of them "don't understand the hype" and think they can sing better than me. Of course, there are more good comments than bad, but I still think people need to find better things to do with their time.

I wasn't expecting all this hate to come along with all the love.

"We're here." Luca puts a hand on my shoulder, snapping me out of my thoughts before I could spiral too far down. I could use a drink.

No, stop thinking like that.

But it would help just a little bit with my stress; it has in the past.

Right now I have bigger fish to fry though, as I walk up the stone stairs; I'm going to be meeting Insieme's manager.

Instead of reaching for a bottle, I reach for Luca and Tony's hand as we climb higher and higher and reach the doors. I stare at myself in the glass door- my curly hair is diffused nicely and my pale pink dress is flowing freely above my knees. I feel beautiful because Luca tells me everyday. Because people comment saying they wish they looked like me. Because I finally believe that I am good enough.

I let out a big breath before pulling on the door handles. Here goes nothing.

"What the-?" I try pulling on the door again, but nothing happens.

Tony scoffs under his breath and raises an eyebrow at me. "Giovanna, sometimes I wonder." He pushes the door open with ease, getting a laugh out of Luca.

"I'm glad you find my struggles funny," I mutter as I follow them to the elevator.

Luca looks over his shoulder and smiles. "Everytime I FaceTime you, you're always reading a book."

"Yes, I'm glad we can agree that you interrupt my free time." I love when he calls me, who am I kidding?

"So how could you not read the *push* sign?"

I drop my lips into a scowl as we step into the elevator. "Whatever."

Tony selects the fourth floor, as instructed by the email from Samantha, and we stand in silence. All three of us are rocking back and forth nervously on our heels, none of us brave enough to make idle chit-chat anymore. Our future is waiting just one hallway away.

After what feels like forever, the door finally opens, and we are off to meet Samantha. We get lost a couple times down the narrow, cramped hallways, but eventually we find a secretary, who guides us into Samantha's office.

"Welcome, you guys! I'm so glad you got here safely," she says, motioning for us to sit down.

Tony was right. To say Samantha is beautiful would be an understatement. Her straight blonde hair surprisingly has no tangles and looks as though she's wearing extensions, but she's not. She's super tall compared to all five feet of me. Whatever shred of confidence I had walking into this room has now disappeared.

"It's nice to finally meet you," I say, trying to swim above the wave of anxiety that has started to come over me.

"Same to you! I've been looking at you guys for a while now, and I'm super excited to see what we can do together." She opens a drawer and grabs what I assume is our contract and hands each of us a copy.

My hands are shaking as I try to read over the words. My voice is no longer working because I have absolutely no words to describe this feeling. My dream is coming true.

"As you can see, you will be with Reen for five years under contract. Once your contract is up, we will meet again and discuss Insieme's future. Before I go any further, I want to make it clear that we need to get an album out to the public as soon as possible while your fanbase is still hot. We need to hop on this quickly before it is too late and people forget about you."

I don't think I can write that many songs quickly because "I Was Wrong" came to me in the car, but we could make it work. I just hope that I can make something everyone will like. I don't want to disappoint anyone.

"You will be spending a lot of time in the studio because we need to write songs and record them. You'll be spending most hours of the day in the studio."

My head snaps up, taking my eyes away from the blurry sheet. "How long are you thinking, roughly?"

She forms her lips into a pretty smile. "That all depends on you, Giovanna."

"Huh?" I blurt, and Tony swats at my knee with big eyes. "Sorry, what do you mean?"

"No need to apologize," she assures me. "From what I've seen in the comment section, you were the one who wrote the song, is that correct?"

"Yes." My voice is so small I want to punch myself. I need to show her that I'm strong enough to handle this.

"Now, we need you to make about ten or more songs for an album."

Beside me, Luca lets out an excited gasp. "That is amazing! I'm super excited to get cracking on this album."

I quickly shake my head. "But what about school?"

"What about it?" Samantha asks.

I tilt my head to the side, shouldn't she know this already? "We're enrolled in online classes. We promised our parents..."

"No, dear, you need to drop those because *this* is your future now."

"But-"

"That shouldn't be an issue," Tony inturpus. I whip my head to him. How is this not an issue? He looks at me with wide eyes, silently telling me not to blow this. Now is not the time or place to argue with him, but he'll be getting an earful from me as soon as we're out of this building.

I keep my arms angrily on my chest for the rest of the meeting. Samantha ran through our contract, and it seems like Reen will do everything for us, which is nice. Very nice of them. Almost *too* nice.

Luca nudges me to stand up and we all shake hands with her and tell her we would be in touch. Tony and Luca seem ecstatic, but this all seems a bit... much.

"We cannot drop out of school," I say as soon as we're inside the elevator.

Tony sighs, annoyed. "Giovanna."

"Don't," I snap. "What if this doesn't work out? What if they're just wining-and-dining us right now? What if this all comes crashing down tomorrow and we don't even have a high school diploma?"

What if, what if, what if.

My breathing picks up, coming out in sharp breaths. I need to call someone because my rational reasoning is falling onto deaf ears. I need to talk to Mary, I'm sure she'll understand me.

"Gia, what did you expect?" Luca whispers so softly, I barely hear him over the pumping blood in my ears.

"I expected- I didn't think... I wanted to finish school."

"And go on tour?" He raises a curious eyebrow at me.

I bite my lip and look down. "No. You don't get to convince me to drop out of school right now."

Luca shrugs. "I know it's scary, but this is how we grow."

"What if it-"

"Stop," he says, taking my hand in his. "Everything is going to work out, I promise."

This is what I've always wanted, but I didn't realize how much I would have to give up and how much it would push me out of my comfort zone. We haven't even been here a week.

This isn't as easy as my dream was.

I need a drink.

But things are different from my dream because I've actually been kissed and Luca and I are together. That isn't enough for me to drop out of school, though.

"Look, you guys can decide if you want to stay in school or not, but I promised my family that I would finish high school, and you know I always keep a promise. I will not drop out of school. That is final."

If there's one thing my parents taught me, it's to always keep my options open. I just don't see how Samantha can expect me to drop everything after one meeting with her, but if the boys don't see anything wrong with that, that's not my problem.

I may have moved out here, but I will stay true to who I am no matter what. I won't let someone else make choices for me.

Chapter 4

I THINK IT'S SAFE to say that I bit off more than I can chew yesterday. The building, the contract, and meeting Samantha, it was all too much. On top of that, the boys were so passionate and eager to sign the contract, it was difficult to look them in their gleaming eyes and tell them I was not going to drop school, but it had to be done. I told them I would be able to handle doing both, but I honestly feel like I have no other option.

That's the reasoning behind my decision to pick up this blue pen and sign my name on my contract. My hand trembles a bit as I scratch my signature onto the paper.

"Congratulations, Insieme!" Samantha exclaims and extends her hand out. I'm the last to shake her hand because the boys couldn't stay in their seats any longer, but I made sure to keep my shake firm like my parents taught me. Maybe if my handshake is firm enough, it will look like I have some sort of idea of what I'm doing. This way it seems like I'm confident.

"Thank you so much for this opportunity," I say with a bright smile. "I cannot wait to start working with you."

She returns my smile with a much prettier one of her own. "The feeling is mutual. I'll send you guys all the information about where the studio is and what time to arrive. For now, have a great rest of your day and I'll see you tomorrow!"

She seems in a hurry to get us out of there, but I choose to ignore it and run after the boys.

"This is fan-freakin-tastic!" Tony practically yells. "Tomorrow we will get to be in the studio, and start recording 'I Was Wrong', and then we'll get to hear our own voices on the radio."

I force out a smile. "It's so exciting, but aren't you nervous?"

Tony throws his head back and groans dramatically. "Can't you just enjoy this moment?"

"What do you want me to do? We can't even have a party or something to celebrate." We're still only 16.

"We could bring the party to us…" Luca suggests with a gleam in his eyes.

"No. I'm going home and doing my *school* work," I say.

I don't know how to feel right now, but I just know that I need to balance school and singing. We haven't even started, and it's already a lot, but I'm too stubborn to admit that to the boys.

I slam my laptop shut and yank on my curls. This hotel room is too small to try and understand math, especially when the boys are blaring music. I can't seem to understand what's going on in the lesson, nor do I really care because I'm trying to come up with song lyrics at the same time. I don't know if the boys even like writing songs because I wrote the last one, but I sure hope they help out because I'm at a loss when it comes to math and song writing.

"What even is this?" I curse under my breath, stomping over to the small table and taking a seat with the boys. "Math will be the death of me."

Tony hands me a bag of chips, which I devour in about twenty seconds. "Nevermind about that, we need to come up with some songs for tomorrow."

"Have you gotten anything from Samantha?" Luca asks, staring at me with such intensity I feel insecure. Is something on my lips?

"No." I shake my head. "I'll keep an eye out and keep you updated, though."

Luca shrugs. "We were also sorta depending on you to write the songs…"

I bulge my eyes out. "What?! Why?" I can't do this by myself.

Luca stares at his feet. "We just thought that because everyone loves 'I Was Wrong', they would love your other work."

I stare blankly at the boys, trying to keep my cool and not let them see just how much I'm freaking out. *You wanted this*, I remind myself. What did I expect? "Okay."

"I'm glad we came out here," Tony says suddenly, getting all serious like he always does. I don't think I've ever met anyone who can go from joking to having a deep conversation in a matter of minutes like Tony does, but that's what best friends are for. Speaking of best friends, I need to call Mary.

"Thank you, Gia," Luca whispers, taking my hand in his. "We wouldn't be here without you."

I shake my head and blush, raising my shoulder. "I already told you guys that it was *you* who made this all possible. You never gave up on me."

Tony runs a tired hand over his face. "At the end of the day, we're here, and I will not waste this opportunity."

"All in, balls out," I agree.

Luca spits out his teeth with laughter. "Classy lady I got myself, hey, Tony?"

"I've been rooting for you guys since day one," he snickers.

Luca gives my hand a squeeze and yawns. "Let's go to bed, and tomorrow let's go get everything they said we couldn't have."

He remembers my prep talk? The one I gave them at our first performance. It's crazy how we blew up from posting a couple of videos, and the fact that he remembers what I said makes my heart swell with glee.

"Luca," I hush into his ear, "I love you."

Chapter 5

"I'M REALLY EXCITED, MARY. I just wanted to check in and see how you were doing though." Mary encouraged me to get on that plane and take a chance, and I'm forever grateful for that. She was always willing to give me that extra push or lend me a helping hand, and that has not changed since I've moved out.

"I'm excited for you!!" I can hear her smile through the phone. "I've been managing back here, but it has honestly been a lot since you've been gone."

"Are you okay?" I ask, sitting down on my bed.

"I mean, yeah. I just really miss you and it's just weird having my best friend being so many miles away from me. We went from seeing each other everyday to nothing."

"I know." I really do miss her, honestly. I miss everything about home; I miss being comfortable. "I miss you too, but I have to do this. I would hate myself for the rest of my life if I just walked away from this right now."

"I'm not telling you to walk away from it, I would hate you if you did," she laughs. "It doesn't make it easier knowing that you're going to be famous though, if that makes sense. I know that you're bound for success- you always were- but I still miss you."

I really needed to hear those words; she always knows what to say when I need it the most and I love her for that. "I'll try and visit as much as possible," I promise. "I will do everything in my power to call you everyday."

"Life gets busy, especially when you're a superstar," she says, and I can picture her smirking.

"I know." I roll my eyes as if she can see me. "We're actually about to head to the studio in a few hours for the first time. I'm so pumped," I express. "We can finally record songs, isn't that awesome?!"

"It is. It really, really is," she says, without an ounce of jealousy in her voice, just pure pride in her words.

"Sweet mother of..." I clamp my mouth shut. I don't know what I was expecting, but it definitely was not this gigantic room. I thought it was going to be like, I don't know, a closet like you see in the movies.

"Don't even think about touching anything," Luca warns, looking at Tony and I. We shrug but don't argue because the amount of times we've trashed Luca's house is way too many to count. We don't mean to, of course, we're just clumsy.

Samantha talks for an hour about each device in the studio, but all of her words go in one ear and out the other. There's just so much terminology that I didn't even know existed, so how am I supposed to know how they work?

I try to focus on her words, but my mind keeps telling my eyes to look at the microphone. It's nothing like the one that Tony has back home; I'm not used to fancy microphones. I've dreamed about recording my work and now I'm looking at all the equipment my favorite singers use. I could not be happier.

"So can we start recording?" I blurt out, shocking myself a little.

Samantha chuckles as if it's a silly question. "I need to introduce you guys to the producer."

"I thought you were our producer?"

"No." She smiles that model smile. "I'm your manager, sweetie."

"Right." I laugh it off, but I'm sure the boys don't miss the sudden flush of red my cheeks have gained. I feel stupid, she talks as if I should already know that.

"But they won't be in until tomorrow," she continues, "so until then, we can sit and write some songs."

Tony sits down at a table that is in the middle of the room and scrolls on his phone, Luca following in his footsteps.

"Do you guys have any ideas?" Samantha asks, sitting down next to Luca. Jealousy flares up like a burning candle in my chest, but I try to push it down. She is so much prettier than me; why would Luca want to stay with someone like me when he's sitting next to someone like her?

I plop down next to Tony, trying- and failing- to keep my face neutral. "I don't usually sit down and write a song," I explain. "It doesn't come to me like that. I have to be in the heat of the moment."

Despite telling her this, she still makes us sit at the stupid table for three hours. Three. I don't even have a single word written down. The only thing I'm thinking about is how I'm missing the Blue Jays game right now. I pull my phone out in hopes that I can stream the game, but Samantha shoots me a disappointing look and I think better of it.

"We got nothing."

"Thanks, Tony," Luca snaps. I look at Tony with wide eyes, both of us equally scared of Luca whenever he gets hungry.

I lean back in my chair, extending my arms all the way back until I hear that satisfying crack in my back. "I think we should call it a day."

Samantha shakes her head. "I don't usually let my clients go until we have at least some ideas down." Luca groans and puts his head onto the table dramatically. I feel his agony. "But." He springs up. "I will make an exception for today because I know you will come up with great things tonight."

"Thank you so much," Tony is saying, but Luca and I can't get out of the studio fast enough.

"See you tomorrow." And with that, Luca and I sprint out of there and flag down a taxi. We're all hungry. We're all tired. We're all homesick.

My leg bounces anxiously as we sit in silence on the ride to the hotel. The thought of my family always causes this weird feeling to arrive in my gut. Everytime I close my eyes, I see them having to give their signatures on statements to even let us move out here. The sight of my mother crying, my father trying to calm her down even though it was breaking his heart to let me go. I'm still their little girl, and I know they want me to chase my dreams and do what I love, but it's still rough.

I let out a sigh, and get no reactions from the boys. They don't even wait for the taxi to come to a complete stop before jumping out, leaving me to pay the driver and stumble out of the car. My legs have become jello from sitting all day.

Luca already has the Jays game on- I don't even try to hide my blush when I see the television- and Tony is rambling off his order for room service. Tony lets out a bunch of "yeps" until finally he hangs up the phone and throws himself onto the bed.

I can't help but feel the weird tension going on between the three of us , no matter how hard I try to focus on the game. I can't take the silence.

"I'm sorry I couldn't come up with anything today," I say, but get nothing in return. Luca is too

busy looking at his hands and Tony is too busy
doing something close to nothing. Great. "I'll try
and come up with a few lyrics tonight so we have
something for tomorrow."

"Sounds good." Luca's voice comes out
harsh, but for the sake of my sensitivity, I choose to
believe he's just hungry.

Maybe if I just had a drink, it would get my
creative juices flowing...

There's a knock on the door and Tony nearly
breaks the door with how fast he flings it. Tony
brings in the trays- a steak for himself, a burger for
me, and a chicken caesar salad for Luca.

"You know, you're not training for spring
football anymore," Tony comments, already stuffing
his mouth with his well-done steak.

Luca shoots his eyes down to his small
portion. "Old habits, I guess."

I eat in silence, thankful for the burger to
keep me company. I thought moving out here with
the boys would mean we would have a lot more fun.
Maybe homesickness is too fresh for all of us right

now. We don't even have the energy to bicker back and forth. We just simply eat in silence.

I finish my burger and grab a pen and napkin and close the bathroom door behind me. The tile is cool and rigid against my thighs, but I need to be alone. In the safety of being alone, I let all of my tears out, staining the brown napkin with each tear. I'm still just a kid, this is all too much.

I tip my head back and squeeze my eyes shut, trying to drown out the millions of thoughts running through my head. I run my fingers through my messy curls and try to breathe. I picture my family at the airport and how I didn't want them to let go of me, but I wanted them to let me go and do this all the same.

I snap my eyes open and scribble down my thoughts onto the tear-stained napkin.

I know I said I want this, and I'm sure I still do

But I want nothing more than to come back to you

And I think the same thought I had when I wrote "I Was Wrong": *this could work.*

Chapter 6

SAMANTHA ASKED US TO meet at the studio two hours before the producers show up, so here we are bright and early. I don't know why I'm breathing like I just ran a marathon, but the sight of seeing the boys and Samantha pass my napkin back and forth makes me want to curl up into a ball and hide.

"Do you have a name for it yet?" Samantha asks, setting the napkin down and indicating for me to write the song on an actual sheet of paper.

I pick up my special pen and title it "In Between", and Luca leans into me. "It's perfect," he whispers. "Thanks for getting it done."

"You're welcome," I peep. He's so close we could kiss.

"Please don't be mad at me," he starts, causing my heart to thump rapidly against my rib cage, "but I think the next songs should be a bit…" He pauses, unsure if I can handle it or not.

"Say it."

"Happier."

"Okay."

"Gia-"

"Understood."

Happier? If he thinks he can make songs *happier*, then maybe he could pick up a pen and write a song. Luca takes the pen out of my hand and makes me look into his eyes, the silence swelling up between us. I huff, "I just write what's on my mind."

Luca puts his hand over mine. "I'm sorry you're feeling like that."

"There's no need to worry, I'm fine."

"But the lyrics…"

"I'm fine."

"*I want to be back with you and be safe// Please get me out of this place*," he reads from my paper. "That doesn't sound like you're 'fine'."

"I write what the fans want to hear. They loved the first one, so they're going to love this one because it's along the same lines. We can add an upbeat drive in the background to lighten the lyrics up a bit."

Luca smiles softly. "That sounds like a great idea." I can tell that he wants to push further, but he just keeps staring at me without saying anything.

My leg bounces as he turns around and I let out a sigh of relief. I just don't like opening up to people, even Luca. He already knows about how much I miss my grandmother, how I used to be so self-conscious about everything I wore and everything I said, but he's also helped me tremendously and I hope he can say the same for me.

"Luca." He turns around instantly. "Can we go outside for a bit? I need a break."

He already has his hand in mine and leads me through twists and turns of the wide hallways. When we're finally outside, he doesn't say anything. That's one of the things I love about him- he always listens before speaking.

"I'm scared this won't work out and that I will have to go back home; everyone will know I'm a failure," I whisper. I know I'm not as famous as other people, but I'm known enough for people to recognize me on the street. People like Diana could come up to us at any given time, so I keep my voice low.

"Aren't you worried?" I ask, a tiny bit of frustration coming up because this is supposed to be the part where he says he understands, but what he says comes way out of left field.

"No." He stares at me with his lips set in a firm line and repeats softly this time. "No, I'm not."

"How can you be so sure?" *Why can't I be this confident?*

"The key is to just take it one day at a time. I have no idea if this is going to work out the way I want to, but I know that we are good. We are really, really great. You wrote a brilliant song and you're still so young, this is only the beginning." He steps closer to me and bends his head down. "At what point do you get over yourself, Gia?"

I think it's a rhetorical question, but when he raises his eyebrow at me I quickly scramble for an answer. "I don't... It's-how?"

"A little confidence won't hurt you, Gia." I nod because he's right. "So let's go back in there, meet with the producers, and I don't want you to second guess yourself because this is what you were meant to do. You're the girl with a dream, remember?"

I straighten out my spine and roll my shoulders back. "I needed that, thank you."

Samantha seems even more professional and careful than usual as the producer runs through our contract.

"Thanks, Mike," she keeps saying. She's even more nervous than I am; I guess if we don't get a producer, we won't be able to even meet our contract agreements with Reen, so her job depends on this just as much as ours.

He tells us what he's all about and who he's produced music for in the past, and I still can't believe that some of my favorite singers have the same producer as I'm about to have. Luca is right: no more second guessing. So when Mike slides the contract to the three of us, I don't even hesitate as I give my signature in blue ink. I don't even answer him when he asks for questions or concerns because I'm trusting Luca's advice on this one.

"It was a pleasure meeting with you," he says as he stands up. "I know that this work relationship will evolve into some sort of friendship outside of the contract." He tosses his head to the side, his blond hair barely moving due to all the gel that he put in it. He continues to ramble on about how excited he is to see our work, and you know what? I'm excited too.

When he leaves I realize two things: one, I have myself a record deal. Two, I need to get to work.

Chapter 7

FOUR MONTHS HAVE PASSED and I can say that I know the hotel menu by heart. I'm also happy to announce that I have been writing song after song- and yes, I've made some happy ones too. Everything is working out between Reen and the producers, as well as with the boys and I.

"I have super exciting news!" Samantha says, nearly jumping out of her seat.

"What?" The three of us ask simultaneously.

"We have a set list and dates for your first tour!"

I nearly choke on my water. "This is great!" I match her energy. "I can't wait. When do we start?"

Her smile only grows. "We will be starting in about a year and a half." My posture deflates. "But that all depends on when you guys are ready to release your album."

"We haven't even recorded the final take of the songs," Tony comments.

Samantha nods her head. "Now that you guys finished grade ten, we can spend more time in the studio."

"But summer only lasts so long, plus I've started summer school to get a head start," I blurt, receiving a sharp look from Luca and Tony.

"This is true, and the boys and I have been talking…"

I don't even hear what she says next because I thought we had open conversations with Samantha. I thought I was included in discussions about everything because that's how it's always been. Why was I not included?

Luca shakes my shoulder a bit, bringing me back to the conversation at hand. "Sorry, can you repeat that?"

Luca says it this time, his voice soft and almost pitiful as if he's talking to a baby. "We don't think this is going to work if you continue with online school."

"But-"

"We can always go back and get our diploma, but this deal only happens once in a lifetime. You have to realize that"

I give him an unimpressed frown. "I get that this deal means a lot for us, but I've already sacrificed so many things to come out here, but I will not sacrifice my education."

"I know that moving out here was overwhelming, and now that you're getting used to it, I think it's safe to say that this is our future," Tony interrupts.

"It's not that I'm second guessing this, because I would love to get a release date for our album and go on tour, but once our contract is up, what happens then?"

No one seems to have an answer for me, so I continue, "I feel like it would be smart of us to keep our avenues open in case this only lasts five years."

"We'll figure it out then, but you have to understand that this won't happen unless we drop school," Luca says, his big eyes pleading with me.

I've given up my family, dance, *everything* to come out here. Some would say that I have nothing to lose, but don't I have everything to lose?

"If you want to go back home, you can," Samantha says evenly as if she's dealt with this thousands of times before, "but I wouldn't walk away from all this when you've come so far in such a short amount of time. Think of all your fans who will be disappointed if they don't get that album."

What is it with people talking to me like I'm a baby these days? "I understand." My tone comes out sharper than intended. "Excuse me for wanting to finish high school."

"We need to act and we need to act now," Tony inputs. "If we don't commit to this, Samantha says she can't hold out for us any longer and we won't get a secured release date that we're looking for."

"So no album without full commitment from us," Luca reiderates.

"I said I understand," I huff. I can feel the tears start to pool at the corners of my eyes, and I'm not even sure why. It just feels like I'm finally at the end of a chapter and it's bittersweet.

It started off as a stupid dream, and I would be lying if I told you I went to bed peacefully every night since. I haven't had a good night's sleep because I can't help but wonder how much simpler my life would be if I never had that dream in the first place.

That dream brought me so many things, though, and I'm so grateful for it. I would not have Luca, Tony, or even this deal. Insieme is my life now, and I have to accept that. No matter what, Insieme has always been and will continue to be my number one priority. I will do whatever it takes to hear my name chanted by millions of people around the world, to do music videos, to do commercials, to do whatever it takes to get my message out into the world. The world needs my songs.

I take a sharp, shaky breath before I say, "Ok."

"Thank you, Giovanna." Luca brings me in for a tight hug. "If this all falls down, I want you to know that I will take all the blame."

I give him the biggest smile I can muster to try and hide my nerves, but it probably just looks like I'm constipated. "It wont." I gently place my hand on the back of his neck. "This will all work out." I try my best to push my doubts to the back of my mind for the sake of the boys.

Tony comes up behind me and puts his hand on my shoulder. "Let's go show the world who we are."

My smile turns into a genuine one as I envision our future. I can see it now: the flashing lights, the fans, the parties. "I'm excited."

That much was true.

Part Two

Chapter 8

"DO YOU HEAR THAT?" I ask breathlessly, trying to slow down my breathing. Tonight is our first concert and it is safe to say that I am a messy ball of emotions. I am nervous, of course, but I'm beyond excited all the same. I always think it's good to be a bit nervous before big performances- at least, that's how it's always been for me.

Although it took a lot of sacrifices, I feel like Insieme has started to make it in the singing industry. Our debut album *Workin'* hit the top thirty in the charts and stayed there for four consecutive months. Of course, this didn't just come from pure luck, this also came from us promoting on social media any chance we could and getting our name out there.

"I can't believe this is really happening," Tony whispers, bringing us all into a huddle.

"Do you realize that we are history in the making?" Luca asks brightly, his beautiful smile shining brighter than any spotlight in this LA stadium.

Things between us have been good- really, really good. I've never been in a relationship where it's lasted this long, we're nearly two years into it. It's been the best, even though we argue sometimes. He understands what I want simply by looking into my eyes; I don't have to say a word for him to know what I need.

"We already are history," I point out. One thing that I had to realize if Insieme was to take off like it has, I needed to gain genuine confidence. I had to fall in love with our work and myself, and I have. I had to believe that there was no way for us to lose.

We get swarmed by a hurd of the backstage crew who run wires down our backs that attach into our ears.

I can feel my adrenaline surging through me like a rushing river. It's times like these when I could use a drink to ground myself and keep my nerves in check.

"Gia, are you okay?" Luca hushes, standing as close to me as possible. He's grown quite tall over the past year or so. Unfortunately, I haven't grown since the fifth grade, so I'm starting to develop neck problems from looking up at him all the time.

"It's just all so real." I match his tone, which only causes him to bend down until his ear is near my mouth, waking up butterflies in my stomach.

Luca laces his big hand into my tiny one and rubs his thumb over my hand. "I know, but isn't it amazing?!" His low volume is now long gone and I'm certain everyone in the crowd can hear him. "Hey, if it ever gets too much for you out there, just look for me and I'll be right next to you."

Just looking into his sure eyes brings a wave of calmness over me. "I needed that, thank you."

"I know, and I love you."

I blush and cock my head to the side. "You look amazing," I comment, running my hand up to his tie knot and tightening it.

Our costume designers thought it would be a great idea to color coordinate our outfits. Luca is wearing jet black dress pants, a baby blue button up shirt, and a black tie. His hair looks like he just rolled out of bed, but it actually took an hour for the hairdressers to get it to sit in a sloppy, messy look. He doesn't look like the boy I first met anymore, but whenever he opens his mouth about ice cream flavors or sports, the little boy starts to come outside of his grown man shell.

"And what about me?" Tony says with a laugh, approaching us with his big smile worn proudly.

"Looking good as usual." I purse my lips and nod my head. He's got the same outfit on as Luca, but in reversed colors. Tony wears black pants, a black shirt, and a baby blue tie. It's not something he would normally pick out in the store- but then again we haven't gone shopping in a while because we will get swarmed by the paparazzi- yet he looks handsome.

"I love this dress," Luca says, not bothering to hide his eyes going all the way down and back up my body. The boys look like sharp-dressed men, but I look like a child because of my height.

"Me too," Tony adds. My dress is the same shade of blue as theirs, and it sits just above my knee. It has black lace at the top, but it's plain on the bottom, and a strapless sweetheart neckline that makes me look like I have a defined collarbone.

"You guys are on in ten," Samantha informs us, coming out of nowhere.

I can't stop my hands from shaking and I try Tony's method of deep breathing, but I won't feel *truly* calm until I have a drink. That's just not an option right now, so putting all my body weight onto Luca's strong body is what I resort to. He drapes his arm around me and places his hand on my bare shoulder.

"I guess we're really not in my basement anymore," Tony whispers, nervously biting down on his lip.

"It's amazing," Luca says. "That we've come so far in such a short amount of time. I mean, we went from singing One Direction to making our own songs."

"Our parents are in the crowd," Tony announces as if we didn't already know that. "It makes me want to puke."

"Tony," Luca scolds, nodding his head towards me and gawking his eyes out.

"Sorry," he mutters. "Everything is going to be okay."

I'm the baby of the group, which I'm grateful for most of the time. They always watch what they say around me because they want to keep my anxiety to a minimum, which I appreciate, but sometimes it feels like they forget I'm the same age as them. Whatever they can handle, I should be able to as well.

Samantha marches over to us and has to scream over the intro music for us to get into our places on the platform that will rise up. We practiced this a thousand times yesterday, but I still shake in the knees and internally panic, wondering if I'm standing in the right spot. I give the boys one last smile before I hang my head for dramatic effect so I can look up when the beat drops.

As I shut my eyes and feel the bass of the intro music pumping into my bloodstream, the world goes quiet. There's no excess noise, just the music living inside my body. The platform rises at the same time my stomach drops.

Chapter 9

THE BLINDING SPOTLIGHT SHINES on me and I raise my microphone to my dry lips. The cheers from the audience is sheer background noise for me right now because I've never heard my heartbeat this loud. I can see the microphone shaking in front of me, but I just can't seem to keep my hands still.

My eyes are clouded with happy tears as I sing the opening lines to our hit song "In Between", the song I came up with when I was crying on the bathroom floor.

I can feel my dress clamping to my legs with sweat as I sing, until Tony takes over at the bridge. I glance over at Luca and he flashes his angelic smile, and I can't tell if the louder cheers are because of Tony's voice or Luca's smile. Probably Luca.

"Yeah, and I'm not saying that I don't want this// Because this lifestyle, I can't resist// And I know I look like I have it all together on your scReen// But when it comes to staying or leaving, well I'm in between," we sing the chorus together,

Luca takes the main melody and Tony and myself harmonize. We try to split our parts up as equally as we can, but it all depends on the lyric and our voice style, and what Samantha and Mike deem necessary.

The drums and guitars die down once the song is over, but the crowd is still buzzing with wild energy. I can't help the laugh that comes out of my lips as I read a sign that says "Will you marry me, Luca Fonzo?" Luca places a hand on my shoulder as he comes up behind me and I point to the girl (who can't be over 13) holding up the sign.

Luca smiles to the ground and shakes his head. "How are we doing, Los Angeles?" Screams. Claps. Cheers.

"We want to thank you all for choosing to spend your Saturday night with us," Tony adds, taking over just like we had practiced. "We wouldn't be standing up here if it weren't for you. For that, we are greatly appreciative."

"We have a great show for you guys tonight, and I know you all want to hear more songs," I say, getting a collective *YES* from the fans, "but we wanted to share some information with you." The crowd goes silent and I hold up my hand to shield my eyes from the spotlight. "I don't know where they are, but our families are here in the crowd tonight."

"We want to give a huge thank you to them for making all of this happen. We are just the singers, but they are the back-bone of Insieme; without them we are nothing," Luca says for me because everytime we practiced this speech, I would get choked up.

"Enough with the sappy talk, Luca," Tony teases, getting a rumble of laughter from the crowd, and from me because Tony is freestyling at this point. "The fans want to hear the songs, *I* want to hear the songs, so…"

He's cut off by a single drum beat, and then two beats. Three. Tony starts singing "Too Good to be True", another song off our album that everyone loves.

"We shared so much//And now we barely say 'bye'// So many questions// But you left me neglected// Maybe it was too good to be true// All the 'I love you's'."

It's got a driving beat in the drums, making up for the sad lyrics. It's just easier for me to write depressing songs because, well, I don't know. It sells though, and that's making Loath Labels happy, which is keeping Samantha and Reen happy, so we're happy and employed.

We sing nearly all the songs off our album at the concert, and the buzz I'm getting off of the crowd is powerful. All of these fans coming to see us- how is this my life now?

I want this buzz for the rest of my life; I don't want to leave this stadium. As the boys stand on either side of me and we simultaneously bow our hands to the floor, I know that this high will soon be over and will be replaced with a higher one when I see my family.

We can still hear the chants of our name when we slowly get lowered down the platform, and then that's when I start sprinting. I quickly disentangle myself from the thousands of wires on my body before Luca clenches his hand in mine. We dash hand-in-hand together, Tony trucking on our heels, and we hop into the tour bus surrounded by security guards that are waiting for us outside the exit doors.

"Todd!" We exclaim once we see our favorite driver. He gives us a smile and barely waits for us to buckle our seatbelts before he puts the pedal to the medal.

"That was..." I can't seem to find the right words to describe this feeling because it's more than one thing. Amazing. Extraordinary. Surreal. "Dope."

Luca spits out his teeth with laughter and wipes a tear from his eyes. "That's what you came up with?"

"I've been saying it for two years now. You've got yourself a classy lady, Luca," Tony wheezes. I swat at his side, but this only escalates his laughter even more.

Being in this bus, laughing- even if it's at my expense- makes me feel *happy*. When I first moved out here, it was so overwhelming and nothing seemed to make sense. Everything came at me at once. I knew nothing. I was running off of the hope fumes in my gas tank, and if Samantha didn't get us signed as quickly as she did, I would have run out of gas way earlier. I'm glad the boys filled up my tank.

Luca clears his throat, silencing Tony and I. "I wanted to let you know that Vince is coming over."

I squeeze my eyes shut and let out a heavy sigh. When I fling them open, Luca is still staring at the floor. "Why?" I ask. I really don't want to see him and have his negative energy in our house.

Tony looks at the two of us with a preprelexed look on his face. "What's wrong with Vince?"

Before Vince went to university, Tony and him got along pretty well- at least, that's what it seemed like at banquets. What I've heard him say when he's on the phone with Luca, well, he seems different.

"Vince has his…" Luca starts.

"Opinions," I finish.

"On our career choice."

"Yep."

"Strong opinions."

He said a lot about us dropping out of highschool to pursue Insieme. I guess he had only heard about our YouTube videos and thought we intended to just post a couple times and go on with our lives. Vince didn't want Luca to risk everything, he wanted him to finish school.

I don't think I'll ever forget the day he called Luca when we had already moved; I could hear him screaming through the phone. He made Luca cry, and it was left up to me to comfort him until he was okay.

"Ohhh," Tony whispers. "Wait, so why is he showing up then?"

Luca shrugs his shoulders. "I guess he wants to spend as much time with Lorenzo as he can." I know it breaks his heart to say that, but it's probably true. "My parents kinda forced him."

"Luca, you have so many supporters," I say. "I mean, did you see the crowd tonight?"

"Someone wants to marry me," Luca jokes, tossing his head to the side and brushing away his imaginary hair to the side.

I nudge him a little and giggle this stupid, little sound that only he brings out. "I guess I have some competition."

"And don't forget the million other twelve-year-olds who follow him," Tony adds.

I shrug. "I did it when I was growing up, it's understandable."

"Me too," Tony says. "Sorry, but can we just talk about how frickin' amazing that was?" I smile and let him continue. "I loved being up there, and did you see how involved the crowd was?"

"We made it," Luca says, his voice full of hope.

We really did make it.

Chapter 10

I DON'T THINK I'VE ever seen Luca this frantic about hosting company. Don't get me wrong, I'm absolutely sweating buckets, but not nearly as much as Luca. He's rearranged the snack bowls at least fifty times in the last ten minutes.

"Will you quit shaking?" Tony asks me, looking at my leg.

"No."

"Relaxxx."

"No."

He folds his arms and squints his eyes. "Everything is going to be fine."

Luca, even though he's as nervous as me, says, "If you can perform at your own concert, I'm sure you can handle this."

It's sweet- it really is sweet that he's trying to calm me down when he's losing it, too. It's understandable why he would be nervous to see Vince, and for me, I'm nervous because I *know* my parents were not happy that we dropped out.

I told them that it wasn't really my decision to make anymore, and I could hear the disappointment in their voices. They always taught me to stick to my beliefs and stand up for what I think is right, and the fact that I just blew over like a blade of grass in the wind made them upset. More disappointed than upset, but it wasn't a good feeling. We would call each other here and there, but it was awkward and unnatural. Of course, with every call that passed, the tension eased up a bit, so now I just hope they were proud of me when they saw me up there.

The doorbell of the tiny house we're renting out rings and the three of us jump up. My legs are shaking and are liable to give out at any moment, but I force myself to open the white door. What will they think of me? I just don't want them to be disappointed.

"Giovanna!" My dad doesn't even wait for me to open the door all the way before he wraps me into a bear hug. My cheeks squish into his chest as he rocks me back and forth. The tears are spilling out of my eyes like waterfalls, and I don't even care.

I forgot what it felt like to be in the safety of my dad's arms. I've grown up in a short amount of time and I've had to fend for myself, but at the end of the day, I need a hug from the person who guided me every step of the way.

I reluctantly let him go and my mother is quick to squeeze me. She's crying way more than anybody in the room, but for once, I decide to bite my tongue and not make fun of her. I owe everything to her. She raised me right, and I'm very lucky to say that because I know some people aren't as fortunate as me. She is my rock. My family has always had my back, even when we didn't see eye-to-eye.

Antonio has this wicked smile on his face as he reaches out his hand for us to do our signature handshake. Clap, clap, fist bump, fist bump, and a *tss* sound with a snap at the end. Basic, I know, but it's our thing and it's special to us.

"I've missed you guys so much," I say. I'm such a weeping mess that it's starting to get embarrassing, especially when I notice that everyone is looking at me. Luca looks concerned, Tony looks like he's holding in his laugh, and Lorenzo looks down at me with a smirk.

"You grew!" I exclaim, craning my neck up so I can see him. He's now a lean and lanky kid, with bird feathers starting to form above his top lip.

"Yeah, I can't say the same for you..." The silence is brutally loud. I stand with my legs wider than my shoulders and straighten my arms. I drop my lips and flare my nostrils, trying my best to hold in my laugh, but of course I fail. Lorenzo gives me a hug and I lead everyone into the family room.

"This is for you," Giancarlo says. He looks older, his hair is now almost completely gray. I know that dark, deep, olive green colored-bottle anywhere. "You could put it in the fridge for now or..." I gladly take the bottle of champagne from him.

"I'll get the glasses, it's time for a toast anyway." I'm already picking up my pace to the kitchen and then turn on my heels and head back towards Giancarlo. "Thank you, and it's so good to see you." I give him a quick hug and he follows me to the kitchen.

"It wouldn't be right if we didn't toast," Giancarlo says.

"Ain't that the truth, G."

"How have things been?"

I hand him twelve glasses and find a bottle opener that should be here in one of these drawers. "It's crazy out here." I smile to myself when I find the opener and hand it to him. "In a good way, of course, but I miss being home."

Giancarlo opens the bottle with a satisfying pop and I'm practically salivating. It's been so long, and I've honestly missed toasting to Insieme. "I can only imagine what it's like for you guys, and in my mind, you guys are still this tall." He drops his hand to just above his knee.

I watch as he carefully pours the bubbly liquor into the tall glasses. My stomach fizzes just like the tiny bubbles in the glass. "There are good days and there are hard days," I babble on, mostly to stop myself from staring, "but I wouldn't trade this for anything."

"It was one hell of a show, Giovanna," he comments, finishing off the last glass. I put all the glasses on the biggest plate I can find and balance it on the palm of my right hand.

"What's your favorite song?"

He doesn't hesitate. "'I Was Wrong'."

"Really?" I scrunch my nose up. "I mean, thanks, but that was the first song we wrote and I think we've improved quite a bit." Even though it made it on the album and is doing well, other songs have topped it in the charts, and I'm not surprised.

He places his hands on the counter and I reluctantly place down the plate and lean against the counter as well. "Look, Giovanna, I've seen my son develop through my phone screen for two years now. You guys keep growing, the fans keep growing, and your talent is obviously growing…"

"But." There's always a *but* that needs to be said, so I say it for him.

"But I like 'I Was Wrong' because it feels like the true Insieme."

"What do you mean?" I raise my eyebrow, shocked at his words. Have we changed that much, and does he mean that in a bad way?

"Wow," he recovers quickly. "I didn't mean that in a harmful way. I just meant that I was the one who recorded the video that blew you guys up, and you're in your uncle's restaurant, and you guys are so young. My point is this: you guys had the talent before you had the fan base. Never forget that."

I smile and look down. "I know what you mean."

"I've never seen my son so excited, and when he calls me, I can hear his smile through the phone. I can hear his smile when he's singing whenever I turn on my radio. I guess what I'm trying to say is, you guys are doing a great job, but it was the first time I knew you guys would make it."

"And here we are." I open my hands to the tiny house.

"Cheers to that."

He didn't have to tell me twice, I was already grabbing the plate and making my way back to our families. Feeling calm in the presence of so many guiding hands.

Chapter 11

IT WAS UP TO me, naturally, to do the toast. I honestly kept it short and sweet so I could finally have the sweet taste of champagne back on my tongue. After I said "cheers to us" and all that good stuff, Luca decided he wanted to add onto it.

"I think we can all agree that Insieme is a walking miracle, and that is true to a certain extent," Luca announces, standing up now. "But it is by no miracle, or luck, or fait, or whatever you want to call it, that we are on our first tour. It is because of Giovanna." Blood rushes to my cheeks and I can't help but gush. Everyone nods in agreement, but I've already made it clear to the boys that they have just as big a role in this than I do.

"Gia, it is your drive that keeps us going everyday. I know I've said this before, but I truly am the lucky one in this relationship, and I love you. So yes, here's to Insieme, but also here's to you, Giovanna Rossi." His smile meets his eyes as he raises his glass to his lips. I don't know how to react; even though our relationship is very public, I still find it awkward to show PDA in front of our families. I don't know. I still love him, but I don't say it back, all I do is smile and take a big gulp from my glass.

I forgot how much I liked it. How my body gets this tingly feeling that starts at the tips of my toes and goes all the way up to my head. I feel like I've been rushing all day and shaking with nerves, and that single sip just grounded me. I take another sip. And another. Before I know it, I'm making my way into the kitchen to pour myself another glass, not really paying attention to what Anna is saying.

I can tell it's Luca who follows me because I recognize his heavy footsteps, so I don't even flinch when he comes up behind me and wraps his arms around my waist. "Hey," he whispers.

I put down my glass and lean my head to the side so I can look at him. "I love you too, you know," I murmur.

"I know."

"Hey, did you see that text from Samantha about the interview she landed for us?" I ask.

He drops his head and walks to the other side of the counter to the snack bowls. "I did, but I don't want to talk about work right now." His tone is surprisingly sweet. "Tonight is a celebration of Insieme. Of you. Of us."

I grin and rub the back of my neck. "You're right, I'm sorry."

"That's pretty great we can do interviews now, hey?"

"I don't want to talk about work."

We burst out laughing and I find my way back to his arms. I find my way back to my safety blanket. I sink my head further into his chest. He plants a soft kiss on my forehead.

"How's Vince?" I instantly regret that I asked it because his smile is now wiped clear off his face and replaced with a sorrowful scowl.

"I haven't talked to him."

I look at him and raise an eyebrow, and then I turn and pour myself another glass. I finish it in two big sips.

"Let's go talk to him," I declare, pouring myself a third cup. "Do you need a refill?"

He looks at me for a long time with an unreadable expression before he says, "Yes, please." I refill his and smile as I loop my arm into his, we're a perfect fit.

"Let's go talk to Vince."

"But, Gia, I don't-"

The champagne has given me this boost of confidence, and I'm walking too fast and I'm too stubborn to stop dragging Luca along with me. I mean, who does Vince think he is? He's in my house, he can at least greet us properly.

"Hi, Vince," I say sharply, my voice slicing through the air and silencing everyone. I put on the fakest smile I can muster. He hasn't said anything to my face, but he made my boyfriend cry, so yeah, we have an issue now.

Vince scrunches his eyebrows just like I've seen Luca do a hundred times. "Hello, Giovanna."

I didn't expect the room to go silent, but I can't stop myself now. "Are you enjoying everything?" I widen my smile even more after I take another sip from my drink. I can feel Luca tense at my side.

"Yeah…"

"Really?" I close my eyes and tilt my head back as I sigh. "Because your brother provided it for you and you couldn't so much as say thank you to him."

I hear Lorenzo let out a snort, but he is quickly silenced by Vince's death stare. I shrug and take another sip. I take another confidence boost. I've missed this feeling.

Vince just sits there with this smug look on his face, and dammit I've seen that stupid look on Luca's face too. They could pass for twins. "I don't know what you think you're trying to accomplish right now," he finally comments.

I feel Luca brush my elbow, trying to get me to walk away, but I've spent too many hours staying up and calming Luca down to let Vince get away with it. "I just want to know what your issue is."

Vince scoffs at me and stands up. He's towering over me, and I would be lying if I told you that I wasn't scared out of my pants, but I don't even tremble. Thank goodness for champagne. "Excuse me for not being a big fan of my brother dropping out of highschool."

"Vince, I told you that we have a contract-" Luca starts.

"For some *girl*," Vince finishes with a sneer, looking at me up and down. "You see, I can't seem to wrap my head around this." He motions his hands in a circular motion at Luca and myself. "The fact that my brother left football and school all behind for *you*."

I try to keep my lips set in a firm line as he carries on. "And what happens when this is all over? All the concerts and tours, then what will you do with your life? You have no back up plan."

I hate to say it because I was so ready to rip his head off a few minutes ago, but he's right. He's right and I've always been worried about that. What happens when our contract is up? I've put all my eggs into one basket, and I'm truly just holding onto my dream now.

I'm so lost in my own thoughts that I don't see Luca punch Vince until I hear the sound of his knuckles meeting Vince's jaw with a loud snap.

"Hey!" Tony yells instantly, but Luca doesn't stop. He picks up Vince by his collar and hoists him against the wall.

He isn't screaming, but his whisper is harsh all the same. "If you ever talk to her like that again, you won't be able to stand straight ever again. How dare you come into our house, attend our concert, and sit there and sulk in your jealousy and say those awful things? Our mother sure as hell raised me better than that."

Vince still has that smirk on, as if he's amused by all of this. As if he's amused by Anna clasping her hand over her mouth and trying not to cry. "You wouldn't get this upset if you didn't know I was right."

"No, Vince, I'm getting upset because I'm in love with Gia and you can't accept that!"

Am I not good enough for Luca?

"That's enough," Giancarlo yells, slamming his hand down on the couch. Everyone but Luca jumps at the sound. I look at my family with wide eyes, and they have the same expression as I do: what just happened?

"Let me go," Vince says, calm as ever.

Luca's hands are shaking with rage as he continues to bunch Vince's shirt into his palms. "Get the hell out."

"Luca, come on," Lorenzo pleads. "I haven't seen you in years." My heart breaks when Lorenzo's voice cracks. I started this all, and now I'm feeling sorry for myself? I'm pathetic.

"You aren't welcome in this house, Vince. Do me a favor, when you hear my voice on your radio, turn it off. When you see my face on the cover of all the magazines, throw them out. When you see any commercials we're in, change the channel."

"Already do," he whispers with a satisfactory smile on his lips.

"We'll come back tomorrow," my dad says, stepping in between the brothers now, forcing Luca to let go of Vince.

I want to cry out and tell my family to stay with me because we haven't talked in so long, but the tension is too high right now. It's as if someone has tied a rope around my throat and won't let go of their grip on it.

I bite back tears as I hug everyone except Vince goodbye. I squeeze as tight as I possibly can before my brother shuts the door behind everyone. As my family leaves, they take a little piece of my inner child with me. We're not who we used to be.

"Luca, I'm so sorry." I don't recognize my voice. I can't even finish what I want to say because I'm choking on a river of tears. Tony catches my eye and he looks like he's uncomfortable.

"I think you two need a moment alone, I'll be in my room if you need me," he announces and trots off, leaving Luca and I alone.

Luca's breathing is heavy and clipped. I don't know what to do, so I just sort of stand there twisting the gold bracelet Lorenzo gave me all those years ago nervously around my wrist.

"I told you I didn't want to talk to him," he finally says, his voice so low I barely hear him.

"I know and I should have listened to you," I respond. "I'm so sorry."

He looks at me with tear stained eyes, breaking my heart in two. "He's my brother." I get to him fast enough before he collapses onto the floor and I hold him in my arms. "Gia," he whispers, "how could my own brother do this to me?"

I can't relate to him because Antonio has always been my best friend, and that makes me cry even more because I'm so thankful for such a great brother. I start crying more because Luca deserves an older brother like Antonio. "I'm sorry, Luca."

"I thought he was supposed to be happy for me," he continues, his words hardly understandable through all his sobs. "I don't understand why he can't just be proud of me and congratulate me."

I run my fingers through his soft hair and put my lips to his ear. "He's been in your shadow his whole life," I whisper. "I know he feels like that because I've felt like that before and I've said things I shouldn't have to the people I love the most."

"But how does he look up to me if I look up to him?"

I rock him back and forth and tip his chin so he looks me in my eyes. "Luca, everyone wants to be like you. You are it. You have *it*. You just have this presence to you that makes people instantly drawn towards you, and that scares him. You are here now and look at all the things we've accomplished."

"I know," he says. "I get that we are history in the making, but I'd trade all the approval of millions of fans for Vince's approval in a heartbeat."

"I know," I whisper. "But, Luca, you don't have to beat him up."

"He hurt you."

"I'm fine."

"No you're not."

I sigh. "This isn't about me."

"I love you so much, Gia," he hushs. "I will do everything I can to protect you."

When his lips meet mine, I can feel the sparks fly between us. His mouth is desperate on mine as he rolls on top of me, becoming my safety blanket again.

"I'm here for you," I assure him through kisses.

"Always," he agrees. "How about another drink?"

I kiss him again and let him take my hand in his and lead me to the kitchen. We clink our glasses together and he wraps his hand around my waist.

"You make me the happiest man alive, so here's to us."

Cheers to that.

Chapter 12

"YOU GUYS ARE STILL UP?" Tony asks, rubbing the sleep from his eyes.

The room is spinning and I'm seeing two Tony's and three Luca's. There's this buzz that's fallen over me, and I love it.

"Dance with us!" I exclaim over the blaring music.

"How much have you had to drink?"

I start to count on my fingers. "One... Two..."

"Gia." He shakes his head.

"I don't know, I lost count," I admit with a laugh.

Tony sighs, "What are we going to do with this one."

"Oh, please, Luca is just as gone as I am."

Luca finds this funny and comes up to me with big eyes and a smile. He puts his hands on my face and smirks. "Keeping up with you, *darling*."

The laugh that escapes my lips is horrendous and obnoxious. "Did you just go all cowboy on me?"

"Possibly."

"Oh, boy," Tony huffs, "I have my hands full. Could you guys get off the couch?"

Luca jumps off with ease and opens his arms up for me to jump into. I fall into him and he wraps me up into a hug. We sway to the music, his eyes never leaving mine.

"I'm going back to bed," Tony announces.

My jaw cracks when I drop it into a perfect circle. "What? No, come on, we're just getting started."

"It's just like old times," Luca adds, struggling to stand up straight.

Tony looks between the two of us skeptically. "One more hour."

"Yes!" Luca and I shout at the same time, getting a laugh out of Tony.

I don't know how much we have, but all I know is our families brought us six bottles and we still have four, so tomorrow shouldn't be too bad. Tony has been dancing on top of the couch for a solid forty-five minutes, and he refuses to come down.

"You're going to break the damn thing," I reason with him.

He crosses his arms and lifts his chin, nearly hitting the light fixture in the process. "I like it up here." He poses like he's at a disco part in the 1970's.

"You need to go to bed."

"I thought you wanted me to stay," he says

"Why are you crying?"

"I don't know!"

"Oh my goodness," Luca mumbles, shaking his head, his wavy hair brushing against his eyes.

"Why are you crying?" I repeat, laughing uncontrollably.

"It's not funny!" Tony cries out.

"You're a crying drunk!"

"I'm sorry I'm sensitive," he says in a sarcastic tone, wiping away his tears and flashing us a smile.

"I knew you were faking it!" I croak. "I love you."

"You little piece of…" Luca trails off.

"No, but seriously, I'm going to fall on my face if I don't get some shut-eye," he says, yawning way louder than necessary.

"Goodnight," Luca and I say at the same time again.

"You two are so cute, finishing each other's sentences and thinking the same thing, it makes me want to puke."

"Leave before I make you clean up," I threaten.

"See you tomorrow." He salutes and runs off.

"Let's just leave the dishes for when we wake up," Luca suggests. "I just want to lay down right now, I don't feel so good."

He grabs two throw pillows and plops them on the floor. He lays flat on his back, wiggling up and down to try and find a comfortable spot on the huge area rug. He looks like an adorable kid, trying to prop his pillow behind his neck so it's just right.

"Do you have something against couches now?" I groan as my hip cracks when I lay down next to him.

"Glad to see you still have old-lady bones."

"Shut up," I whisper. I rest my head on his chest, our breathing matching instantly.

"*Amore*, I could lay here forever."

Butterflies start to come alive in the pit of my stomach when he speaks Italian. "Me too."

"You looked beautiful up on stage," he hushes. I can feel my eyelids starting to get heavy with every passing blink, especially with Luca's warm body pressed so close to mine.

"I know," I joke.

He doesn't even regard my comment, I look at him and I can tell that his mind is elsewhere.

"Don't listen to Vince," he whispers after a short pause. "Please, don't."

"Luca." I bring my hand up to his cheek. I really, really don't want to talk about his brother right now. To be honest, I would be happy if we could just lay in silence and fall asleep in eachothers arms.

"I can't stop thinking about it," he continues.

"Luca, I know it hurts, and I will be with you every step of the way, but you need to get some rest."

He scoffs, "I can't sleep, Gia." I can't see them, but I can hear the tears in his voice. "How can I sleep when I know my own brother hates me?"

How do I respond? I don't. I press my body closer to him, in hopes to comfort him. I give him a soft kiss, and at first he doesn't kiss back.

"I get it. Let me know what you need," I hush.

He searches my eyes with a soft expression. "You. I need you." He gives me a passionate kiss, one where it makes time freeze as if you are in the middle of a picture frame.

"I've always needed you," he murmurs against my lips. "It's you and me against the world, *amore*."

"And Tony," I add with a smirk.

"Insieme."

I've been feeling homesick, but I haven't felt this at home since moving out here until now. I'm happy- whether it's the alcohol in my system, Luca wrapped around me, having my first concert, or seeing my family- I'm truly happy.

I'm not thinking about what song to write next, if there's going to be a scandal tomorrow and I'm going to fall on my face, or if I looked silly out there hitting a high note. For the first time in a while, I fall into a heavy sleep.

Chapter 13

SNAP. I SLOWLY OPEN MY eyes to find Tony shoving a camera in Luca and I's face.

"You guys are so cute," he says in an extra high voice.

Luca basically shoves me off of him and brings his knees to his chest as if he's scared. "What the hell?" I ask. Now I'm cold.

"Last time we fell asleep and Tony took our picture, well, you were in the washroom for a solid hour," he explains. "I will be damned if you puke all over me this morning."

I smile at the memory of our first sleepover. Who would have thought we would recreate that photo a year later?

"I'm older now," I defend, trying to smooth out some of the wrinkles in my shirt.

Tony flips his phone over so we can see his screen, and all the articles published on the front of magazine covers are absolutely true, we really are the cutest couple in the world.

"You'll break the internet if you post that," Tony says. "But I am so ready for it to blow up."

I deleted all the posts of Danny on my Instagram, but they still managed to make their way into the entertainment media because the paparazzi love to stir things up every chance they get.

I lift my shoulders and drop them. "Fine, let's post it." I upload the photo and immediately throw my phone onto the coffee table.

"I can't believe you guys passed out on the floor, what's wrong with the couch?"

My eyes go wide. "That's what I asked him!"

"He's always been a bit... different."

"Yep."

Luca rolls his eyes and slowly stands up, observing our tiny house. "What a mess." He rubs the temples of his head and lets out a sigh.

I scoff at him. "You created it, Mr. 'I-just-want-to-dance-all-night-'."

He stacks four plates on top of eachother and shakes his head. "You really fought me on that one, hey."

I smile and shake my head, biting my lip. "Fine, turn this on me."

"Fine, turn this on me," he mocks under his breath. I spring up and glide over to him. I don't know how to describe it, but it's like when I'm with him, I don't notice or care about anything else. I know that my phone is blowing up with thousands of notifications, but he's the only thing I see. He's like my river, constantly pushing me forward with his caring current.

"What should we do today? We're hitting the road tomorrow and we have to pack tonight, but what are we going to do until then?" Tony asks, getting up to help us with the dishes. We have a system: Tony brings the dishes to the sink, I hand wash all the dirty dishes because Luca thinks dishwashers will damage the plates, and I hand them to Luca, who drys them and puts them back neatly in the cupboards.

"I was thinking about going out for lunch with my family," I say.

"With all of us?" Luca asks, his eyes silently pleading with me. He still doesn't want to be one-on-one with Vince, and I can't say that I blame him.

"Well..." I really want to catch up with my family.

Tony's phone buzzes viciously in his pocket and he nearly drops it when he pulls it out. "It's Samantha." Saved by the bell. "Hello." He immediately puts it on speaker and I shut off the running water and dry my hands.

"I have some great news," she says. My body automatically stiffens whenever she starts off like that. "Your concert was a success, and everyone wants to meet with you. I have about five interviews set up in place that we'll have to fit in between shows, and a bunch of companies have reached out and asked if you would be interested in doing commercials."

It's like the air has been knocked out of my lungs. I hate the word famous, but this feels like the world is treating me as if I'm royalty, but I'm just a normal girl who sings sometimes with a couple of guys.

"Have you been reading all of the comments on your posts?" she asks.

"No," Tony says. "Remember we told you that we don't look at any comments."

Although I don't do it as often as I used to, I still scroll through hundreds and hundreds of comments some nights. I just get curious about what people have to say, even if I feel my heart drop when I see a hate comment. It's funny because Insieme gets so much love from complete strangers who call themselves fans, and I barely remember what they say, but when I see a comment about how ugly I am, or how fat I look, or how we should stop singing, it sticks with me.

"Well, people are going crazy over the picture Giovanna just posted, which is catching the eyes of news articles."

There's already articles about Luca and I, so I'm not surprised at all. Paparazzi is constantly looking for things to latch onto.

"We also have a photo shoot coming up for the next album."

I shake my head and shut my eyes. "Wait, hold on, did you just say next album?"

"Yes…"

"We're still on tour."

She chuckles, "That doesn't mean you stop working. I suggest you bring a pad of paper and a pen on the tour bus to write some songs because as soon as this tour is over, we need to release a second album." She's talking as if we should know all this.

"Isn't it a bit soon?" Luca asks.

I swallow down my anxiety as I say, "It takes me a long time to write songs."

"Insieme has a healthy amount of momentum right now, and if we play it right, Insieme could very well be on top of the world in a few years."

Tony raises his eyebrows and mouths *she's got a point*. Yeah, she has a point, but I want to enjoy my time on tour.

"I'm not asking you to be in the studio for twenty three hours everyday," she says.

"Really? You're not going to tell us to drop out of highschool again?" I wish I could bite my tongue, the silence is deafening. The only sound that can be heard is my heavy breathing. She can't expect to overwork us and get away with it, can she?

"Is there something you would like to say, Gia? Are you not enjoying your time on stage? How was it when the crowd screamed Insieme's name? How does it feel to step out onto the street and hear a thousand cameras go off? How does it feel to get over one hundred thousand likes on your pictures in less than ten minutes? Did I really force you into such a *terrible* life?" Her words slice me like a knife.

"I didn't mean it like that. I meant... I don't..." I can't find the right words to describe how I'm feeling. I know that I sound so spoiled, but I thought touring was supposed to be stress-free.

"That's what I thought," she says, satisfaction dripping from her words. "Let me put it to you this way: Insieme is climbing a very high mountain. I stumble across your page and strap you all up with a backpack with everything you need. Now, you are not at the peak of your full potential, but you are getting there. I need you to allow me to do that; I need you to trust me."

Tony and Luca look at me as if I need to say anything to her, but I remain silent and stare blankly at the phone. She's blind if she can't tell that I already trust her, considering I dropped out of high school for her.

"I will see you early tomorrow morning, and don't be late. Yes, Gia, I'm talking to you." She hangs up before we can even say goodbye.

"I'm going to head to my room," I say sheepishly. The boys don't stop me as I bolt out of everyone's presence. Suddenly, it feels like the air is heavy on my chest and every breath is a struggle.

I reach into my pocket and dial the only person who I know will distract me. I wait. One ring. Two rings. Three rings. "Hey, this is Mary, sorry I couldn't answer your call…" I wait for the beep.

"Hi, Mary, it's Giovanna. How are things? How are you doing? I really miss you; I miss home. Now that I'm leaving you a message, I realize I really don't know why I'm calling you. Anyways, have a good night? I don't know, the time change messes me up, call me back if you have a chance."

I shrink in my skin, bunching my hair up into fists. I don't even know why I'm being so dramatic, this is what I've always wanted. It's just that my family and I barely got to talk last night. I'm on tour and I don't even know what I'm doing. Samantha is putting a lot of pressure on me, and my best friend isn't picking up my phone call because she's busy moving on with her life. It seems as though everyone is getting on with their life.

Everyone except me. I feel like a scattered, immature kid. No amount of dresses, no amount of money, and no amount of fame can take away the uncertainty of my future. It's like I'm walking a tightrope without a safety net to catch me, it's all or nothing.

I don't want to be overworked, but I also know that Samantha is right- people will forget about us if we don't constantly come out with new work. So I sit and I cry all my emotions out, now a blistering headache from the hangover and tears come over me. I stare at my teddy bear and reach for my grandmother's necklace around my neck to soothe me. I remind myself that I am doing this to make them proud as well, so I do the only thing I know how to do when I'm feeling overwhelmed with emotions: I head to the kitchen, grab myself a bottle, and I write our next single.

Chapter 14

"HERE'S WHAT I'VE COME up with," I
announce, making my way up to Samantha's aisle
and I plop down next to her. The tour bus is huge-
someone could live here. Tony took the back of the
bus, I took the middle section, and Luca is close to
the front, and of course, Samantha is directly behind
the driver's seat. This morning, I was complaining
to the boys that I didn't end up seeing my family
last night, but this tour bus seems to be making up
for it. I snap a couple of shots and send it to my
brother, telling him that I'm literally living like I'm
in a movie.

There's beds, booths, and there's even a bar
filled with bottles for Samantha and the crew, but
I'm sure there will be a chance for the boys and I to
sneak back there.

She doesn't even look at the page for a
second. "Too sad." She hands it back to me, not
looking up from her phone. This woman is always
on her phone, usually talking to industry people.

"Excuse me?"

"Look, you're lucky that Luca- and Tony, but mostly Luca- had the idea of masking your sappy, and quite frankly, depressing lyrics with instruments and driving beats. People pound their first to the beat of the music, but we can't do that with this album."

I narrow my eyes and fold my arms in front of my chest; it wasn't all Luca's idea. "And what exactly are you looking for me to write?"

She stops typing on her phone and looks up at me. "I'm saying that you will lose your fanbase if you keep putting out sad song after sad song."

"So what the hell do you want from me?" Anger is pooling in my gut, and I don't know how much longer I can keep it together before I explode. Who does she think she is? How can she tell me how to write *my* songs?

"You can't keep your eyes off of Luca for two minutes, write about that." She sounds bored, almost annoyed.

"You want me to put out a cheesy love song?"

She tilts her head back and sighs, "Giovanna, as your manager, it is my duty to make you successful. Please, shut your damn mouth and listen to my advice. If I didn't know what I was doing, I wouldn't have this job."

I gather up my papers and head back to my designated spot and sprawl out. I stare down at my paper and read the lyrics that spilled out of me last night like a leaky water bottle.

"Going in a million directions// Striving for perfection// Yeah, but I have no idea what the hell I'm doing// I feel like I'm always losing."

They aren't exactly lovey-dovey, but they aren't that depressing. I shake my head and put my papers aside, and without thinking, I turn my gaze to the bar. I sit up a little straighter, looking all the way right, all the way left, and then all the way right again. Everyone is busy doing their own thing.

I move quickly and swiftly with purpose to the bar, quickly grabbing a bottle of vodka and ducking for cover. I take a sip of whatever little water is left in my water bottle and then fill it up with vodka. It's easier than it was at Luca's house.

"Gia," Tony calls. My heart jumps out of my chest as I quickly fumble for the cap and put everything back into place. I make sure the cap is sealed before I shoot up and dash away from the bar. "Come sit with us."

I make my way to their makeshift circle, joining the boys and putting on a smile. I take a drink from my bottle, and all the noise gets quieter. All my thoughts calm down. The nervous buzz is now replaced by a familiar one, a buzz that makes my pupils dilate and my heart beat rapidly against my rib cage.

"I was just saying how much I miss my PlayStation and we should have brought it," Luca says.

I feel like his eyes are piercing through me as I take a drink. "You like to lose, don't you?"

His lips part into a soft smile, red surfacing on his burning cheeks. "I'm not *that* bad."

"I guess you'll just have to prove it."

"I'm good at most things I do."

A blush of my own appears on my cheek and I try to hide my stupid smile with another sip.

"So I was thinking," Tony starts.

"Oh, gosh," Luca mumbles, smiling brightly at me.

"You cost us nothing but money whenever you start off with that," I add, running a hand over my face.

"Oh, yeah? Like what." Tony folds his arms and leans forward, eyes narrowed at us accusingly.

"Clothes, ice cream, pens, home-decor that you could easily find at a thrift store but you must get it for fifty dollars at some designer store." I tick them off one-by-one on my fingers. "Shall I go on?"

He rolls his eyes. "This time is different, and by the way, you never say no to all the things you just listed."

He does find really cute stuff sometimes, but I will never give him the satisfaction of letting him know that. "Anyways, what were you thinking?"

He gives me a satisfied smile and slouches down in his seat. "I think we should hire a choreographer so we could be all in sync during our concerts."

"Absolutely not," Luca blurts almost too quickly.

To be clear, I don't want this either because I think our color coordinating is already borderline cheesy, but I just like to push Luca's buttons. "I think that's a great idea."

"No you don't." Luca makes his eyes grow three times in size, shaking his head.

"Think about it." Tony sits on the edge of his seat, he's so cute when he's excited. "We're all doing our thing and then like during the chorus we could break out into something like this."

"What the hell was that?" I spit out my teeth.

"I saw Justin Bieber do it in one of his concerts," he says, repeating the weird motion.

I scrunch my eyebrows together and drop my mouth. "Are you supposed to be running on the spot but in… slow motion?"

"Yes!" He claps his hands excitedly. "See, you get the idea."

I shrug. "I just don't want to be too cliche, you know what I'm saying?"

I look over at Luca, who has his head buried in his hands. "Wouldn't it be cool, though?" Tony presses. "We can't just be chaotic up there."

"I would rather be chaotic than attempt whatever it is you just showed us," Luca pipes up.

Tony lets out a laugh. "I never said I was good at it. Fine. I guess you guys will win this one."

"Jeez, I was really scared for a second there," Luca says sarcastically.

"Shut up." Tony throws his neck pillow at Luca. They continue to bicker back and forth as I just sit and turn my head back and forth every time they speak.

A pang of sadness hits me as I watch them. They grew up as best friends and know each other from the inside out, and at times like these it feels like I'm intruding a little bit. They don't make me feel that way, it's all in my head, of course, but it really does make me wish Mary were here.

She was always the one I called when something happened; she was always one call away. I told her about everything under the sun, and she told me everything too. She was, and still is, my best friend but things are different now. I'm on tour and I barely have reception out here to call her, and besides, I don't want to bother her because she's busy with her own life.

"I'm going to get some rest," I say to no one because they don't even respond. I get up, making sure to keep my bottle closely tucked under my arm. I make myself comfortable on the bed and close my eyes. I can't fall asleep though, my brain is still working in overdrive.

I can't believe that this is actually happening. I've been in a car plenty of times, but now I'm on a *tour bus* and as soon as I step out of it, fans will come rushing towards us as if a water dam has been broken.

The thought puts a smile on my face, and so does Luca's hand resting on the curve of my torso. "Are you asleep, Gia?"

"Yes," I say.

He laughs under his breath as I turn around to face him. "We're going to stop and get a quick bite to eat." The bus slows down and turns into the parking lot of a 24/7 diner.

"I'll be right there." I'm slow to get up. I didn't realize how comfortable I was until I was forced to step out into the cool night air.

The bright red and blue lights on the diner sign makes me squint, and I'm thankful for my Blue Jays ball cap to keep my face covered in the dark light so I can walk in with ease. I find Tony and Luca sitting already, with Samantha and the rest of the crew at a separate table. I take the booth side, while the two boys sit across from me on chairs.

"Let's see what we have here," I say, picking up the menu and scanning through it. I make a *hm* sound at the back of my throat as I take a gulp of water.

"I wonder what Gia is going to get," Luca whispers to Tony, loud enough for me to hear.

"I think she's going to opt for a salad this time," Tony replies, kicking me jokingly under the table.

I set down the menu and raise my eyebrows to them. "Is there an issue?"

"Hi there!" A waitress appears before the boys can answer. She does the usual spiel about what her name is and that she will be serving us tonight, but she's going too fast for me to even comprehend what she's saying. She's bouncing with energy, even though the diner is practically empty with only about three other tables seated. "What can I get for you tonight?"

I don't even hesitate. "I'll have your classic burger with fries, please and thanks."

This cracks the boys up; they laugh so much they can barely spit out their order. The waitress eyes them suspiciously before turning around back to the kitchen.

"Oh, shut up," I say, rolling my eyes and sinking into my seat.

Tony lets out a dramatic yawn. "I'm so tired."

"I feel like you fall asleep literally anywhere at any time."

"This is true," Luca agrees. "I don't know how you do it. Gia is definitely jealous."

I open my mouth, but Tony quickly interrupts me. "You can't contribute to this conversation until you can go one night without taking melatonin."

I bite my lip and stare at my bouncing leg. "My thoughts keep me up at night." I can feel flames on my cheeks grow.

"Sorry," he whispers.

I can't stop. Once I say a little thing, I have to spill out my guts. "It's just that I'm second guessing every single thing that I do now that so many people are putting me on a pedestal. I mean, what do I know?" I scoff at myself. "How do people look up to me if I don't even know what the hell I'm doing?"

I look up just in time to see Luca and Tony exchange concerned glances. "We all get what you mean, you don't have to explain yourself." Luca meant for it to come out sweeter than it did, I can see it by the shock in his own eyes. He stampers, trying to recover. "I meant- no, that sounded way worse than I intended it to. I was…like, it's hard to explain-"

"He meant that you aren't in this alone," Tony takes over. Luca nods his head aggressively. "We're here for you if you need anything."

I look at my two best friends sitting across from me and take a big, deep breath in and out. The media might have an idea of who they are, but I get to see who they really are and that means the world to me.

Luca nods his head and copies me, Tony joining in. Breathe in, breathe out.

"I'm going to eat my burger," I say as soon as it hits the table, "and then we are going to continue this tour and it's going to be the best days of our lives."

"Here's to making memories as we try to figure this shit out," Luca adds, meeting my eyes and smiling.

"There it is!" I shout, slamming my fist down on the table.

"What?" The boys ask, looking over their shoulders. "What is it?"

I smile and look over at Samantha, who is busy on her phone calling thirty different people, and then I look back at the boys. "The theme for our next album, of course."

Chapter 15

WE TRIED TO HIT all the states on tour, and for the most part we did. Tonight is the last concert in New York, and I could not be more excited. Show after show, I started to get more confident. The big crowds no longer intimate me, I've learned to feed off their energy.

The bigger the crowd, the bigger the show I put on.

Our fan base continues to grow, and our album has topped the charts for six consecutive months. And you know what? We deserve it.

"Gia!" Samantha yells into her microphone.

I snap back to attention, singing softly because I don't want to use all my energy at sound check. I'm clearly behind tempo since I came in late, so Samantha waves a hand and tells us to take five.

We always take thirty when she says that.

"Are you excited?" I ask, jumping up and down.

"You have no idea," Luca says.

Tonight is going to be our biggest show yet. Since it's the last show of the tour and we're in New York, I told the crew I want to "blow the roof off of this place". I'm talking about fireworks, strobe lights, who knows, maybe some flames?

"It's going to be so great!" I squeal. I can't contain my energy.

"You love performing now," Tony comments, taking a big gulp of water.

"Yeah, you really turned a new leaf, hey?" Luca adds.

Yes, I have. I've cracked the code on how to give the best show they've ever seen. Here's how I do it: I notice when the tour bus slows down and tell them I have to use the washroom, as soon as I hear all of the voices fade out, I go to the bar and fill up my water bottle with whatever drink I feel like. I pace myself, of course. I only take a few sips an hour before, but as soon as we get the thirty minute warning, I dash to find my bottle and chug it.

It gives me the confidence to do all the stupid shit the fans want me to do. I sing cover songs, I jump up and down, I shake my shoulders; whatever comes to me in the moment, I do it. I am wild on stage, and the fans can't get enough.

"I love my life," I respond, closing my eyes and swaying to the music that is constantly playing in my head.

"I love to see it," Tony says.

My eyes go big as I realize something. "Oh!"

"What's wrong?"

"Aren't we on the John Feton show in like two days?"

Samantha comes up from behind Luca, grazing his shoulder to get by him. I flare out my nostrils on instinct, a pang of jealousy surging through me. Luca has not been as affectionate with me today, if anything, it feels like he's stepping back whenever I step towards him. It's probably in my head, but why didn't he move or push Samantha off?

"Yes," Samantha says. "We've been approached numerous times to be on the show, but our schedules never fit together until now."

"That's great!" Luca says, smiling brightly at Samantha. I shoot my eyes down. "I'm kind of nervous."

"Why?" I blurt.

His brown eyes meet mine, he looks just as surprised as I feel right now; it's not like me to blurt. "Because I've never done an interview that big before…" He says it like it's obvious.

"And how many concerts have you performed at now?"

"But that's different. In a concert we are singing, the crowd is there-"

"I know what a concert is."

Now I know it's not in my head, he takes a big step back with his arms raised. His eyes go even wider as he searches my face for an answer. I don't give him any.

All tour, he's been too tired for me. He doesn't want to stay up late anymore, he doesn't want to talk so much anymore, and sometimes he doesn't even kiss me.

Tony and Samantha go completely still, holding their breath so they don't upset me.

I glare back at Luca, who's glaring at me now. "What?" I ask.

He shakes his head and turns around. "Piss off," he mumbles as he storms off. He slams the door behind him. Samantha looks between Tony and I for some sort of explanation, but Tony just shrugs and I really don't want to talk to Samantha right now.

I sigh and walk after Luca. I emerge from the doors to find him sitting on the ground with his knees brought to his chest and his head between them.

I plop down beside him, leaning my back against the outside of the building, but he doesn't even glance at me. "I didn't mean to snap at you, I just thought I saw something-"

"I don't want to hear it."

I sit. I let the silence fill up the space between us. I want to tell him exactly how I feel, but it's not the right time.

"I'm nervous because I don't want to sound stupid on live television." He leans his head on the wall. This is weird, we've always been in the opposite position. Luca's always been there for me, it's time I be there for Luca. A guilty feeling starts to rise up inside of me, because Luca has been nothing but patient through my many breakdowns, and I just snapped at him. I wouldn't want to date me either.

"When I'm on stage, I just have to sing. I talk through lyrics and people think I'm the most brilliant person alive," he continues, "but I know I'm going to get nervous and stumble over my own tongue." I write the songs, so, technically, *I* talk to the people through my lyrics, but I choose to bite my tongue.

I run my warm fingers through his soft hair and he lets out a heavy sigh. "I'm so sorry, Luca."

"I know."

"Do you want to hear where I'm coming from?" I ask softly, he nods his head. "Luca, people are going to judge you. It doesn't matter what you say or how you say it, somebody won't be happy. To one person, you'll be their role model, but to someone else, they can't stand you."

"Are you trying to calm me down?" he laughs. "It's not working well."

I chuckle quietly and squeeze his shoulder. "If there's one thing I've learned from this tour, it's that not everybody has to like you. Not everybody is going to like you. That doesn't change how much you love yourself. How much talent you know you have. How much you have to say to the world."

"Look at us," he says. "Usually I'm the one saying this stuff to you."

"Well, I look up to you."

"I look up to you too."

We burst into laughter. "How can you look up to me if I look up to you?" I ask.

"We're screwed," he says between laughs.

"It's all about confidence, Luca. You've made it this far, there's really no possibility for us to lose."

"Thanks, Gia, but why were you so short with me back there?"

I shoot my eyes down. I don't want to make him upset, but I should be open and honest with how I'm feeling. "You barely give me the time of day lately, but you don't seem to have an issue with Samantha brushing against you."

"Gia, you're being a bit ridiculous."

"Am I?" I try to keep my voice low, but I'm failing. "Because there have been *weeks* where you don't tell me you love me. I get that being on tour is exciting and new, but it's like you're forgetting we're in a relationship. When I try to talk to you at night, you are either on your phone or you're falling asleep as I'm speaking!"

"Forgive me for being tired! Why is it me who always has to put in maximum effort? You can take me out once in a while, if that's what you're looking for."

"Luca, it's not about going on dates every night. You haven't told me you loved me in weeks!"

"Giovanna, I'm dealing with my own shit! I don't always have time to babysit you and hold your hand through everything."

"I'm not asking you to babysit me, I'm asking you to treat me like your girlfriend. I have to deal with so many hate comments on my appearance, a little bit of validation and reassurance from you would be nice once in a while."

"What happened to your advice of 'just getting over yourself'?"

"Luca, if we're in a relationship, I expect you to compliment me. I expect you to respond when I tell you that I love you!"

Silence. We're both breathing as if we just ran a marathon, neither of us daring to look at each other. What the media fails to understand is that while we are cute, we get into fights just like normal couples. Sometimes it feels like the fans and the paparazzi alienate us, saying that we are perfect and we have no issues. This is not the case right now, and it sure as hell hasn't been the case for a month.

"Sorry," he says, offering nothing less and nothing more.

"Sorry."

"Hey," he whispers. "I really am sorry."

He leans up and gives me a long, passionate kiss. He bunches my curls into his hands and moves his body closer to mine. His mouth is desperate; I've missed it.

He pauses, breathing heavily into my mouth, his lips inches away from mine. "I love you." His voice is husky.

"I love you, too."

"I'm sorry I've been a bit distant lately," he continues.

I put my finger to his lips and whisper, "It's okay. I get it. Luca, I'm just as much to blame here."

"I should be there for you, and lately my mind has only been on the tour."

I would be lying if I said this tour hasn't taken us out of the honeymoon phase

"I need to be there for you as well, it's not all your fault," I say.

"Gia," he whispers before kissing me again. "Now, more than ever, we have to reassure each other."

I nod. Not only with words, but with actions. "You have a million girls chasing after you."

"You have a million boys chasing after you."

"Life is hard for beautiful people, hey?" I laugh, rolling my eyes.

He pulls me into a tight hug. "So what do you say, tonight we show people what they want?"

"Yep." I look up into his eyes. The tour has changed his face a bit; he's a lot older looking now. His face is more defined, his hair is a little longer, accentuating his waves, I am the luckiest girl in the world.

"Are you ready to headline the news?" he asks with a devilish smirk.

I wrap my arm around his strong neck and return his smirk with one of my own. "Always."

He laughs, touching his head to mine. "I forgot how much you love attention."

I purse my lips and shrug. "What can I say?"

He leans down and plants his lips on mine, and it's like time stops. The world goes still; the only movement I feel is his hands wandering up and down my back and waist. Everything is perfect when I'm with him.

Nothing else matters.

I don't want anything else but him.

All the fame, the money, all of it. All of it means nothing without Luca Fonzo.

Chapter 16

"TONY, I TOLD YOU WE were not doing it!" I have to scream over the opening act as we stand backstage.

"I thought you wanted this show to be the best one yet." He crosses his arms, pouting like a five-year-old.

"That was meant for the crew," I explain.

"And us," Luca hushes, bending down so he's hovering over my ear.

My cheeks go red, a mixture from the alcohol and Luca.

"So what's the issue if we do this?" Tony asks.

"Because you aren't Justin Bieber," Luca says.

"But I really think we can pull this off." Tony demonstrates the move once again.

"That's enough." I place my hand on Tony's shoulder as I laugh.

"Fine," he huffs. "We're going on stage now anyways."

"Yeah, we know, Samantha," Luca says, cutting Samantha off before she tells us to take our places. This woman is always walking as if a bear is chasing after her; always in a hurry, always with purpose. She just smiles and her long blonde hair flips as she turns around, making sure everything goes smoothly backstage.

The rumbling from the crowd starts. My eyes close. My heart drums. Luca grabs my hand. I squeeze back. I come alive.

The platform rises and we're greeted by thousands of screaming fans. The stage is pitch black as the drums beat rhythmically; I can feel the music in my veins. A spotlight shines straight on me, but I keep my head bowed. The fans yell even louder, and I can see neon pink signs out of my peripheral vision. I don't think this amazing feeling will ever get old.

"Looking in the mirror and wanting to change//and so I put my body through pain// I didn't want to be the ugly one anymore// There were nights where I wished I was unborn," I sing.

And I keep singing. I can feel my throat go dry as the night goes on. The crowd gets louder every time the strobe lights go off during a beat drop. The boys and I interact with the audience like we've never done before, shamelessly reading posters out loud, judging their dance moves, and Tony even took someone's phone and we posed for a picture.

I just know *Entertainment Tonight* is going to have a hay day with this one.

To see that something as simple as holding eye contact with a fan and waving at them makes them almost pass out, well, it's a great feeling. It is surreal.

"Ladies and gentlemen, boys and girls, or whoever you are, thank you for coming out tonight," Tony says, heaving some breaths into the microphone.

The backstage crew comes on stage, pushing a three seater brown couch out, and we plop down on it immediately. "Performing really sucks the living life out of you," I whisper, inhaling sharply and receiving an eruption of laughter from the audience.

I sit in the middle of the boys, as I do in most of the photos. Something about strategic placement- I don't know, Samantha tried to explain it to me, but I can't remember much of anything right now. My only focus is feeling this moment.

"Silenceeeee," Luca hushes, bringing a finger to his lips. The crowd obeys, going so quiet that you could hear a pin drop.

Luca picks up his guitar that was sitting beside the couch as he continues to talk. "Gia, Tony, do you know what day it is?" he asks.

I look at Tony and shrug, playing the role we had practiced. "Tonight is our last concert of the tour?" I have to force out a smile to suppress the tears forming in my eyes. While I've had my ups and downs on tour, trying to figure this new lifestyle out was not easy, I've come to love this. I'm going to miss the adrenaline that comes over me as I step on the platform seconds before going on stage and singing my heart out. I'm going to miss seeing fans support us, but I know that there will be many more tours to come, and I can't wait.

Luca starts playing the soft melody of "I Was Wrong", getting claps and cheers from the crowd. "Hey!" he yells. "You're ruining this moment for everybody." The crowd laughs, making Luca rip out a contagious laugh.

He is so cute.

"Yes, Gia, this is our last concert for a while." I don't know why, but when he says my name, it does something to me. It just rolls off his tongue like no one else's.

"I know," Tony says, putting an arm around my shoulder. "Today marks the day that Insieme was officially created."

"Making this night even more special," Luca adds.

"So it only seems fitting that we sing our first song we ever performed in front of a live audience," I say.

The crowd goes wild and Luca doesn't bother telling them to settle down this time. He doesn't have to.

As soon as I raise the microphone to my lips, they go completely silent, wanting to hear us. No one sings along with us this time. We sound angelic. The only sound in this big arena is our harmonies blending together like a match made in heaven. Maybe it's the last concert for a while, maybe it's the memories I have attached to this song, maybe it's the way Luca is staring at me, or maybe it's because I'm so incredibly proud of us, but a tear runs down my cheek as I sing.

The memories come flooding back in. Our sleepovers, the ice cream shop, our YouTube channel.

Danny.

During the last chorus of the song, we stand up, getting a cheer from the crowd. Luca stands as close to me as he can while holding a guitar.

"*I Was Wrong*," we all sing together, harmonizing and drawing out the last line. Luca's eyes meet mine, are we thinking the same thing? The fact that I didn't want to admit my feelings to him and ran to Danny, but I was so completely wrong.

It's not that Danny is a bad guy, by any means. It's just that him and I were more of a high school couple, but I knew that Luca and I would be endgame.

As soon as the music for "I Was Wrong" finishes, the beginning of "No One" by Alicia Keys starts playing. "And we couldn't leave without singing at least one of our cover songs," Tony explains, dancing stupidly to the music. He's the best.

Luca sets down his guitar and picks me up, so I wrap my legs around his waist. The crowd goes crazy, thousands of people are jumping up and down, fanning themselves with their hands.

We are giving the crowd the content they want.

As we sing about how no one can come in the way between us, he doesn't take his eyes off me and I don't take my eyes off of him. He has his hands around my waist and mine are around his neck, matching each other's movements and getting a rise out of the crowd.

Right now, we are Hollywood's cutest couple, although I do feel a bit awkward holding a microphone in one hand the other one is draped around his neck.

At the bridge, I jump off of him and turn around so my back is towards him. He wraps one strong arm around my stomach and pulls me closer, and we sway to the beat. Left. Right. My heart is pounding even louder than the screaming crowd.

I love it. And as we step onto the platform and stop singing even though the music is still playing, my adrenaline shoots through the roof. I don't want to stop performing, I don't want to stop the party.

But as we descend further and further and the thousands of people start to fade away, my heart swells. To think that we started off as a couple of nobodies and now we are selling out stadiums for our tour. I'm so proud.

"Why are you crying?" Luca asks, taking off my earpiece for me and examining me to see if I'm hurt.

I open my mouth, shut it. I'm not sobbing, but I can't seem to stop the tears rolling down my cheeks. "I… just-"

"We're all going to miss it," Tony says, brushing my arm sympathetically.

Luca nods his head in agreement. "This isn't the end."

"I know, but it feels like this is the end of like... I don't even know what I'm trying to say." I throw my hands in the air in frustration.

"The end of what?" Luca asks, a smirk forming at the corner of his lips.

Tony just scoffs as if I shouldn't be so sappy. "This is only the beginning."

Chapter 17

"TONY."

"How the hell does he fall asleep in a *car*?"

"Right before an interview, too," Luca says, shaking Tony again.

"We don't have time for this," I complain, throwing my head back with a sigh.

"Care to help me, *amore*?" Luca asks, making his eyes wide like he always does.

I clap my hands close to Tony's ear as loud as I can manage, finally getting him to jump out of his seat. "Why?!"

"Because we were trying to wake you up for fifty flipping minutes," I say.

"Sure, yeah that's exactly how long it took you to wake me up," he replies.

"Are you two done?" Luca asks. "We were supposed to be with our makeup artist like twenty minutes ago."

"I swear, you guys have absolutely no conception of time whatsoever," Tony whispers just loud enough for us to hear.

The building is surprisingly bland, considering that John's show is flashy to say the least. He has a live band with him, and bright lights, of course, so the plain gray building is a bit of a surprise.

This is it, I think to myself as the three of us get seperated into our own private rooms, *the last part of my dream is about to come true.*

"Hey, darling, how are you?" A woman appears out of nowhere, scaring me and causing me to jump out of my skin.

"Jeez, you scared me," I say, clutching a hand over my chest.

"Sorry." Her voice is sweet, just like her green eyes. She has huge ruby hair, and she's just a little bit taller than me. I'm so used to standing next to Tony and Luca, who both continue to grow like weeds, that standing next to this woman makes me feel sort of normal.

"It's okay, I'm good."

She looks me up and down before patting the hair dresser chair, motioning me to sit down for her. "You don't look too good, sweetie."

"Excuse me?" I give her a look as if to say: *do you even know who you're talking to*?

"You look nervous," she says matter-of-factly, shrugging. She takes my hair out of the messy ponytail I had tied and starts playing around with it. "What would you like to do with this mop of hair?"

"Okay," I huff, sounding all flabbergasted. "I don't even know your name because you have yet to introduce yourself to me, and you are already judging my hair?"

She laughs softly and continues to play with my hair. "The name's Kassie."

"Nice to meet you, Kassie," I mutter.

"Oh, don't be so sensitive. I love your hair, if I'm being honest," she says.

"Thanks."

"So does the whole world," she whispers under her breath, staring into the mirror in front of us. I shoot my eyes down, suddenly self conscious of just how awful I truly look right now. There is no color in my face whatsoever, and with Kassie fluffing my hair bigger and bigger, I look like a train wreck.

I look and feel like death rolled over.

"It isn't easy, you know," I say softly as she starts to wet and shape my hair into a more presentable look.

"What isn't, sweetie?" Concern wrapping up her words as she works quickly.

"Being this naturally beautiful," I joke. And from then on, it's like we've been best friends for ten years. I tell her everything: who I was before the fame, how I got to where I am now, and even how I didn't want to jump into a relationship right away with Luca.

I don't even realize that it's time to get ready to head on stage until she starts packing up her supplies and the boys barely knock on my door before entering my room.

"Shoot," I curse under my breath. "I'm not even dressed yet." I look down at my dressing robe and can't help but smile.

"We know," Luca says. "You are always late."

"At least your hair looks good," Kassie buds in.

I nod as I look at my reflection, meeting her eyes in the mirror. "Thank you," I say.

"You're always beautiful, remember that," she whispers, parting her lips into a gigantic smile.

I can't help but hang my head and blush, shrinking in my skin. "I meant thank you for more than just the hair."

"I know." She puckers her lips together. "It's my job to keep you distracted, or else the nerves will get the best of you."

I can't help but smirk. "You know, I've been on my first tour, and the hair stylist that my management hired is not nearly as good as you, I'm sorry to say."

She responds with a shrug of her shoulders.
"You know where I am if you need me."

I extend my hand out. "It was a pleasure."
She shakes my hand firmly. "If you receive a call
from a woman who sounds like she's in a rush to
get off the phone with you, that's my manager, so
don't hang up."

She just laughs, sounding like a duck having
hiccups, but it's cute. "I'll give you my business
card."

I accept it and feel suddenly awkward. Do I
go in for a hug? Do I just sort of stand there? I don't
know.

"Giovanna, get your ass in your dress,"
Tony demands.

Nevermind.

Kassie looks between me and the dress the
stylists have picked out for me. "You step into that
dress, Giovanna, and you become an icon. So
straighten up that spine and go knock 'em dead."

I raise my chin a little, a flash of pride washing over me. "Let's go knock 'em dead," I repeat.

Chapter 18

"AND THEN SHE JUST passed out," Tony babbles. A storm of laughter erupts from the crowd and John comes within seconds.

John's eyes meet mine. It's different actually being on a set of a TV show rather than just watching it from my couch, but things are going smoothly so far. The boys have been doing most of the talking.

"Can you confirm or deny this?" John asks, his voice significantly deeper than Tony and Luca's.

I flash a smile at the camera. "It's true."

John dramatically drops his jaw, looking me up and down. "You passed out when you saw your view count, but yet you just finished touring?"

"I know," Luca chuckles, "she's a complicated one, isn't she?"

Tony nods his head in agreement. "She's never been the easy kind."

John drops his head, his eyes remaining on me. His salt and pepper hair gleams in the bright lights being shone on us, and it accentuates his oddly smooth skin. "Do they always give you a hard time?"

I purse my lips together and roll my eyes. "Unfortunately."

Another burst of laughter. My heart leaps in my chest at the crowd's engagement.

John clears his throat, straightening the papers on his desk. "So tell me about how your first tour went! Was it everything you expected and more?" His eyes still don't leave me, even when I look at the boys to see who would answer.

Tony answers first, sitting taller now. "It was pretty surreal, and I don't think we even had any expectations going into our careers, but this tour was *awesome*."

John nods his head. "What would you say was the biggest surprise during your concerts?"

"The signs the fans make," Luca spits out immediately. "There were a couple times where I found myself singing and then I would read a sign because, you know, it's on neon yellow paper, and I would actually start to sing the words on the sign."

His laugh stands out against the crowd's. "And some of the things our fans come up with, it's…" he pauses.

"Interesting," Tony offers.

"Exactly." Luca reaches in front of me and high-fives Tony. When Luca leans back, he puts his arm around me, getting a gushing reaction out of the audience and myself.

"That was actually something I wanted to touch on," John says, motioning his head at Luca and I. "It is no secret that you, Luca, are a favorite when it comes to ten-year-old fans." I scoff, parting my lips into the smallest smile. "But yet, you and Giovanna seem to be one of the best, long-lasting Hollywood couples. Is it difficult for you, Giovanna, to know that so many girls want your boyfriend?"

I open and close my mouth. *What am I supposed to say*? "Um, not really." Is all that I come up with. Before the show, Reen gave us scripts of responses to John's already made questions, and we were given strict rules to stick to that script no matter what. No one told us what to do when John asked a question that wasn't there.

"Just to clarify," he says, "I don't think you have anything to worry about."

I lean closer into Luca, subtly resting my hand on his knee. "I think Luca and I keep our personal relationship private for the most part."

Luca nods his head in agreement, but John just looks at the camera and cocks his eyebrow up. "Take a look at this." He looks to the side and points at a small screen while the audience looks at the big screen behind us. The viral video of Luca and I dancing with each other at our last concert appears before my eyes.

I stare down at my tight black dress, my cheeks going as red as my high heels. "Well," I say once the video finally goes away.

Luca sits up taller, clearing his throat. "We're happy, so let's move on."

"So, tell me a little bit of how Insieme came together. Of course, we've all heard the story about Giovanna having a dream, but could you expand on that a little bit for me?" John asks, acting as if he didn't just embarrass me infront of millions of people.

Tony takes this one, noticing the shift in Luca and I's mood. "It didn't really take that much to convince Luca and myself, considering that we were doing nothing with our lives at the time." Everyone laughs for some reason; I think fans just laugh at everything Tony says. "We sort of just clicked right away."

John nods his head, looking back at me again. "And have you found it difficult to be around each other for so long, Gia?"

Gia? Only my close friends call me that. It only rolls off of Luca's tongue perfectly, it doesn't sound good coming from John's mouth.

I swallow the lump in my throat. "Tony is a handful." The audience laughs at my comment, making my smile return.

"Right." He sounds uninterested. "And it must be hard to be in a relationship and be in a singing trio as well. I mean, you're working with someone you're dating, so you're constantly around each other. I can only imagine how many arguments you get into."

Another unscripted question. *What is his obsession with my relationship?*

I feel the anger boiling in me, and I'm trying really hard to keep my cool, but I'm a ticking time-bomb at this point. "Not really."

Luca squeezes my shoulder gently. "We manage just fine."

I'm uncomfortable. Luca hasn't even looked at me for this long like John is right now. When Luca looks at me, he looks into my eyes and tries to read my emotions, or he tells me he loves me. John isn't looking at my face, he's looking at my chest.

I feel stupid in this dress.

I feel stupid sitting here.

I'm melting under his gaze, and not in a cute way.

I think I'm going to be sick.

John seems to leave the topic alone once Luca shoots him a glare, but I just zone out now. I can't even see two feet in front of me because I'm looking through teary eyes. I think they're talking about our new album coming out.

Tony nudges me and I force out a smile. "Thank you," I peep out, and as soon as the camera light dims, I set my lips into a firm line. I can't get out of my seat fast enough. I don't care about the audience, they've seen enough of Insieme today. I need to get out of this building.

I can hear Tony and Luca's dress shoes stomping after me over the click of my high-heels, but I don't bother to slow down. I feel like the walls are closing in on me. My breaths come in short, sharp bursts, and my puffed- out hair is bouncing behind me.

"We can't go yet!" Tony calls out. "Giovanna, wait!"

I spin on my heels. "I need to get out of this place." To anyone walking past, it would look like we are in the middle of a huge argument. They can probably hear me from a mile away; I don't know why I am screaming.

"Calm down," Tony whispers through gritted teeth.

"Don't fucking tell her to calm down," Luca snaps, grabbing me by my wrist and pulling me into his chest. I can't help the tears that pour out of my eyes.

"Shhh." Luca brushes my hair away from my face. "It's okay, I'm here."

"What happened?" Tony asks, moving closer to me and placing his hand awkwardly on my shoulder.

"Didn't… you… see.." I can't even get words out between my tears. I'm trying to breathe to calm myself down, but I'm a lost cause.

"John fucking Feton is what happened," Luca says, breathing angry air out of his nostrils.

"You didn't like the interview?"

"No she did not like the stupid interview, John was staring at her the whole time!"

I bury my head further into his chest. "I hate him."

"And he called her Gia, and only we can call her that," Tony says, trying to recover from his obliviousness.

"Exactly," Luca says, trying to calm down just as much as me.

The worst part is that I watched John's show when I was younger. I dreamed, figuratively and literally, about coming onto his show. I wanted all the glam, the glory, the dresses, and yes I even wanted some of the money, as pretentious as it may seem.

But what I wanted the most: I wanted to be like the people I saw on TV when I was younger. I'm not saying I have to be the next Madonna, but I want young girls to see me and I want to inspire them. I want to inspire them to be different. To be unique.

That's why I have the big curly hair. The full red lips. The gold jewlery. I am different, and not in a superior way, I am just finally comfortable in my own skin. I'm getting to know my style, and I rock it shamelessly now.

And then John just reminds me just how bad society is.

My childhood dreams are crushed.

I snap my head up at the sound of footsteps, immediately tensing and drawing in my breath. "The after-party is in about five minutes, you guys were the last guests on the show tonight." I let out a sigh of relief at Samantha's voice, even if she still sounds like she has people to see and places to be.

"I don't think we're going to stay." Luca isn't asking.

"But it will look better if you did," Samantha says.

Luca clears his throat. "We aren't in the mood at the moment."

Samantha puts her tongue on the roof of her mouth, making a *tsk* sound deep in her throat, and somehow manages to get me off of Luca. "What happened, Giovanna?"

Despite my three inch heels, I look up at her. "Men are disgusting."

She laughs, placing a hand on my shoulder. "Oh, honey."

I drop my gaze down, suddenly feeling stupid that I am surpirsed. "It wasn't even that bad, it could have been much worse, but he just made me feel uncomfortable."

Luca shakes his head. "Don't try and deflect, Gia, it was bad and unacceptable."

"Did you hear the interview?" Tony asks Samantha.

"I didn't, I had an important phone call to take." Of course she did.

"Well, he seemed to be really invested in Luca and Gia's relationship," Tony says, finally clueing in.

"He went off the script, didn't he?" Samantha already knows the answer to her question, so we don't bother answering her.

"The party is this way!" John calls, appearing in the backstage hallways.

I don't look at him, I look at Luca's hands. They're balled into an angry fist, his veins popping out of his skin and his knuckles turning completely white.

I don't even try to stop it. Neither does Tony or Samantha.

Luca marches up to John, who wears a surprised look on his face. Luca doesn't even wait for John to speak, he just plants a hard punch loud enough for everyone to hear right between John's eyes.

"What was that for?" John wails, grabbing the bridge of his nose.

"You keep your eyes off of *my* girlfriend," Luca spits out, shaking with rage. "You're lucky I didn't do that on live television."

John furrows his brows. "What are you talking about?"

"Give it a rest." Luca towers over him, John seems like a fly next to Luca. "You didn't even look at her eyes when you were talking to her, so no, we will not be at your party." Luca starts walking back towards us.

"You're crazy." John has the audacity to laugh.

Luca stops dead in his tracks, turning on his heels and slowly faces John. He reaches John in two big steps and grabs the collar of his shirt and holds him up. "Fuck you."

John tries to look at me, but Luca forces him to look into his burning eyes. "Don't even think about it. If you ever, and I mean *ever*, reach out to us again, we will decline. Just know that I am holding back right now for the sake of not ruining your makeup, but I wish I could rip your eyes out right now.

"You disgusting old man. Are you not embarrassed of yourself? Don't you have a family at home that just watched you stare at the breasts of a twenty-year-old?" He starts to walk away, and then a thought passes through his eyes and he turns back to John. "I always preferred Colton Barker anyway," Luca spits.

Tony comes over to me and wraps his arm around me. "It's going to be okay, let's get going."

Luca is still giving John a death stare.

"Luca, let's go," I whisper.

"Get out of my face." He brushes his hands on his suit pants as if touching John was disgusting, I bet it was.

"You think I'm afraid of some twenty-year-old," John scoffs.

This time, it's me who walks up to him. My eyes move side to side as I examine him. "You know, I really loved you and your show when I was kid." My voice is so low that everyone has to strain to hear me. "And I was so excited to be here, especially since I dreamed of being here before I was even in Insieme." He takes a step back now as I take a step towards him. "You disappointed me."

I can feel the tears swelling up in my throat, so I turn away and the boys and Samantha follow after me. We leave John standing with his mouth wide open. I hope this is the first and last time I will ever be in the same room as him.

Luca is the only one who is able to match my pace, so I intertwine our fingers together. "I love you."

This makes him stop walking, causing Tony to nearly bump into him, but Samantha drags him out of the way just in time and the two of them give us some space.

"I'm so sorry," he whispers, grabbing my waist and pulling me to him.

"You've done more than enough," I assure him. "You have nothing to apologize for."

"I love you so much, Gia," he mumbles, his voice raspy. He leans down and places his lips on mine. Electric sparks radiate off of the two of us.

I need him, he's the weight that keeps me grounded. He always has and always will be my anchor.

"Let's get some sleep." He holds my hand and we walk out of the building to the car.

Tony is already in the car, telling the driver that we just want to go to the house, and Samantha is standing outside of the car, looking at her phone.

"Giovanna," she says, stopping me by raising her hand.

"Yes?"

The boys are already in the car, but I can feel their eyes burning a whole in me as they eavesdrop. "It sucks what happened in there, I'm looking at videos of it."

"Of course, everything is already open to the public," I mutter. I shouldn't be surprised anymore.

"I'm sorry that happened to you," she continues, choosing to ignore my comment. I just nod my head and offer a weak smile. "But, Giovanna." She pauses, making a dramatic face and placing both her hands on my shoulders.

"Yeah?"

"Welcome to Hollywood."

Part Three

Chapter 19

"ANOTHER ROUND!" TONY YELLS at the bartender, swinging his finger in a circle in the air.

"It's on us," Luca calls out.

The music is blasting, I can barely hear my own thoughts over it, let alone hear whatever the fans have to say right now. So many cramped, sweaty bodies pressed together in such a tight space; I love it.

Before I know it, another line of tequila shots are lined up for us on the bar, and Tony is standing on a barstool trying to give a speech over the music.

"I could go on forever about you, Giovanna, but then this party would turn sad." He has to yell, screeching at the top of his lungs, for me to hear him. "You have always been the baby of the group, and to see you turn 21 yesterday, well, it was a lot."

"Is he about to cry?" I hear someone ask.

Tony raises his shot glass in his hand and I gladly help myself to another one. "Ijustloveyousomuch."

"Tony, get off the chair," Luca laughs, holding out his free hand to help Tony down. "You're *pissed*."

"Like you're any better," Tony scoffs, squinting his eyes at Luca.

Luca just shakes his head, rolling his eyes at Tony. "Here's to you, Gia."

Everyone raises their shot glasses and shoots back the tequila.

It burns…

In the best way possible.

I can feel my heartbeat pick up as if it's trying to keep up with the fast-paced music. Yes, yesterday I turned 21, and yes, I am the youngest in Insieme. I'm certain everyone in the club right now knows that I'm like a little sister to Tony because he's been saying it for fifty minutes straight now.

"Wanna dance?" Luca asks, already pulling me to the dance floor by my wrist.

I don't know what kind of remix this is, but I just move my hips to the beat, draping my arms around Luca's broad chest. I can feel his firm muscles underneath his white button up shirt.

I may be the birthday girl, but Luca is stealing the show right now. He's in black pants that fit him perfectly, a white button up shirt with the top button undone, exposing his gold chain that sparkles every now and then. He's gleaming with sweat, but not an excessive amount, it's the kind of amount that looks like he just got out of the shower.

Luca presses his head against mine, having to lean down so he can actually look at me. "You're beautiful."

I smile brighter. I feel beautiful and I actually feel good about myself, especially when Luca gives me that reassurance that I need.

He smirks as his eyes trail to my lips and he bites down gently on his bottom lip. "I love you," he mutters before planting his soft lips on mine.

Time. Stops.

The music becomes background noise compared to the rattle of my heart pounding in my chest. I no longer see the hundreds of people crowded around us because my eyes are shut. It feels like we are the only two in the club right now.

He is the push, I am the pull; our kiss is an even balance.

"Gia," he whispers, pulling away from me.

"Yes." Why am I out of breath?

"Happy birthday."

And that's how the rest of my night goes: Tony orders more rounds, Luca drags me onto the dance floor, I fall more and more in love with Luca, and then he ends up kissing me as if the world is about to end and he can never taste my lips again.

I couldn't be happier.

I stumble to the bar, making sure everything is still in my purse. "Let's head to the house."

"You want to go home already?" Tony asks. "The night is still young."

I stretch out my arms and look around. "T, the ugly lights have come on."

"Shit," he laughs. "Did we close the bar?"

"Sure did," the bartender scoffs. I press my lips together to suppress a laugh and nod my head towards the door, motioning for the boys that we're heading out now.

Our security guards are already waiting for us at the front doors, and Tony climbs into the shotgun seat while Luca and I take the backseats.

"That was so much fun, thank you guys," I say, scrolling through the different photos on my camera roll. I select four of them to post onto my Instagram, making sure that Luca and Tony are in all of them before people get any ideas that Insieme is over. Trust me, it's happened before.

"We wanted you to have a good day," Luca comments.

Tony twists in his seat so he can see us. "We have another present for you."

"Tony!" Luca's voice cracks.

"What!" Tony turns back around and folds his arms over his arms. "I couldn't keep it in any longer." I swear he's three years old.

Luca raises his eyebrows and shrugs his shoulders. "I guess you did keep it in longer than I expected."

"Oh, shut up," Tony huffs. "Anyways, Gia, you're going to love it."

"You guys have honestly done more than enough for me," I say genuinely. I don't expect the boys to do anything for me, putting up with me everyday is enough.

"We do it because we want to."

A comfortable silence falls over the three of us as we look out of our own window. I still haven't fully settled into our house, it just doesn't seem like we live there. Now that we're spending more time in it, I feel like it should have more of our personality, but it remains bland. Tony buys all the expensive decor, but that's strictly for his room. I find it quite boring, so when the driver pulls onto our driveway, a little bit of distaste washes over me.

Tony flicks on the lights, mostly just to latch onto the wall because he can't stand straight right now. "Don't peek!" he exclaims.

"We're not in the club anymore, you can speak normally," Luca says to Tony, rolling his eyes at me.

Tony stumbles back into the family room with a big gift wrapped in blue wrapping paper and hands it to me. "You guys did too much." I can feel the tears welling up in the corner of my eyes already.

"Open it," Luca urges, sitting down next to me.

I tear into the wrapping paper with shaking hands. "Do you like it?" Tony asks.

I let out a sweet laugh. It's a big picture frame collage that I'll end up hanging in my room. It's filled with photos of the three of us, including the pictures we took at Tony's house at our first sleepover. There's the picture we took when we signed our contract, pictures at our first concert, us at restaurants, on the tour bus, sitting on this very couch we are sitting on right now. I love it.

To see myself change throughout the years, to see how much Insieme has grown, in a single picture frame makes me emotional. I don't even bother to hold in my tears anymore.

"Great, we made her cry," Tony mutters, dragging his hand over his face.

I look up at the boys, taking my eyes off the beautiful picture frame. "I love you guys."

"We love you too, Gia."

I give them a bright smile, wiping my tears from my cheeks. "This is the best gift I could have ever asked for."

"You're welcome," Luca says, taking the frame out of my hands and placing it gently on the coffee table. Out of all three of us, he seems to be the most sober one.

Tony can barely stand straight. I can't keep my emotions in check. Yet Luca seems to be aware of anything and everything that is happening around him.

"Look, I hope you had a good birthday and I'm glad you enjoyed the gift, but I am *spent*," Tony comments. "I need to get to bed before I pass out right here, right now."

He stands up too quickly, losing his balance and ending up back on the couch. "Tony, take it easy!" I say, spitting out a laugh.

"Yeah, yeah, see you guys tomorrow." He gets up slowly this time, and eventually we hear the click of his bedroom door.

It must be the alcohol, my hormones, Luca's outfit, or a mix of all three of them, but I've already rolled myself onto Luca, kissing him as if I haven't tasted his lips in five years.

He flips me with ease, positioning himself so I'm completely underneath his body weight. "Gia," he whispers every now and then between kisses.

"Luca," I mumble, pulling back just enough to look him in his eyes.

"Yes, *amore*?"

I blush at the name. "Thank you for making my birthday so special."

He freezes at my words, hoisting himself up onto his palms. "I know how much you miss your family, so I just wanted to do everything in my power to make sure this day was great."

I bite my lip. "It was more than great."

"I'm glad," he chuckles, leaning down and giving me another passionate kiss.

"You know I didn't need all this though," I say against his lips. He pauses, breathing heavily as his lips stay over mine. "I only needed one thing and one thing only."

"Oh, yeah? And what might that be." He gives me a confident smirk.

I snake my fingers through his smooth hair, answering quickly. "You."

"I'm right here," he whispers, pressing kisses up and down my neck every now and then. "I'm always here. You have me wrapped around your finger." I close my eyes and smile. "So have me," he continues. "Take every last piece of me until there is nothing left. I don't need you to leave any leftovers because I'm meant for you and only you."

"Luca," I whisper again, but he keeps speaking as he closes the space between our bodies.

"I want you, Gia," he says, causing the tension between us to rise.

"You already have me." My voice is barely a whisper.

He responds with another kiss. "I love you, Gia."

My heart explodes into a million little pieces. We don't talk for the rest of the night, we keep our lips pressed against each other and our hands roaming up and down one another.

For once since I've moved out here, I feel at home.

Chapter 20

"AGAIN?" I FLING MY EYES open at the sound of Tony's voice. I'm still on the couch pressed tightly against Luca. "This is like the fourth time this week."

"Oh, shut up," I say, pushing myself off of Luca.

"Good morning to you too," Luca says, stretching his arms above his head, exposing a little bit of his stomach as his shirt lifts up.

"Is it not uncomfortable?" Tony asks in disgust, opening up the fridge and looking for something to eat.

I get off the couch, shutting my eyes tightly and rubbing my temples; my head is pounding.

I take the juice carton out of Tony's hand and take a big swig. "Give it a rest, T."

He pretends to glare at me as he takes the carton back. "Find a room," he mumbles under his breath, but I choose to ignore him.

I snatch the juice back and walk over to Luca and hand it to him. "How are you doing?" he asks me, declining the juice with a lazy wave of his hand.

I plop down next to him again. "I have a massive headache," I complain. "It feels like someone is drilling a whole in my skull." I ball my hand into a fist and motion a drill going into my head.

Tony scoffs. "You can stop pretending that this is the first time you've gotten drunk."

Luca runs his hand over his face. "Gia's first time getting drunk with us is not a moment I want to remember." He cringes at the memory of me draped over the toilet.

"Yeah, but I went a little too hard last night," I admit.

"And who's fault is that?" Luca says with a slight smile forming on his lips.

"Yours!" I shoot back. "You and Tony kept ordering shots."

Tony shakes his head. "Oh no you don't. Don't try and blame us now." I can hear the laughter in his voice that he's trying so hard to suppress.

"It's not like we couldn't afford it, though," Luca points out.

This is true. I would be lying if I told you the millions of dollars sitting in my bank account isn't nice. But you know what? We worked for this. We deserve it.

"So I was thinking," I start, but Tony quickly interrupts me.

"Stop."

"Gia, please," Luca adds.

"I can hear the dollars draining out of our account as we speak."

"That's a bit dramatic," I say. " That's Tony's thing, anyway. I was thinking that we should really take a happy turn in the new album."

"Yeah, that's a good idea."

"See, I'm not costing us any money."

"Shocker."

Luca gets up and grabs himself a glass of water. "We're in the studio tomorrow, we can probably get Samantha's opinion on it."

I don't need her opinion, I think but I keep the thought to myself. I'm starting to learn to let Luca say whatever he wants without snapping at him. I'm trying to be better. I want him to feel comfortable enough to say whatever he wants without me biting his head off.

"I was wondering if you guys wanted to start writing some songs as well? Maybe?" I don't know why my cheeks are warming up.

"Absolutely not," Luca says way too quickly.

"Why?"

He returns to the couch, groaning dramatically as he throws himself next to me. "Because."

There's a long pause; I'm waiting for him to elaborate. He doesn't. "Because..?"

He just shrugs and remains silent.

Tony clears his throat, if only trying to relieve some of the tension growing in this room. "If I come up with anything, I'll let you know."

"Thanks for the help, T," I say with a bitter tone directed to Luca before shooting off of the couch and slamming my bedroom door behind me.

I'm 21, for crying out loud. My father claims I'm independent and he's so proud of how well I've been handling myself out here- yes, he gave a speech on my birthday over Facetime, and I'm sure there will be more when I go back home next week- but I still feel like I'm flying off the seat of my pants. It's getting harder and harder for me to come up with something that Reen will enjoy, and the boys are not writing any songs, putting more stress on my plate.

I take out my notebook, filled with scribbles only I can understand. I like my songbook like that though: messy. If you open these pages, it's like diving straight into my mind.

The messy abiss of endless thoughts in my mind is right here on these pages.

I can't even focus on the lines because of my pounding headache, nor do I try to concentrate more. I try to write about partying and what it's like at the clubs and how you inevitably end up with the person you love at the end of the night, but nothing is coming together. They all sound silly and overdone.

Everything I'm writing is stupid.

I feel stupid.

The lyrics are cringey.

If anything, I wrote better songs when I was 16- years-old. But the boys want this. The producers want this. My career depends on the producers and the labels liking the songs I make, so it's not really up to me anymore. I have to write what the people want.

Nobody wants an album with just sad songs on it.

Samantha said that to me when I brought forward a new song, and her words have yet to leave my thoughts.

I draw huge circles on my page, pressing my pen as hard as possible until the page rips right underneath the point of my pen. I slam the book shut and pick up my phone, dialing the only person who I want to talk to right now.

"Hey, Giovanna." Mary picks up the call right away, but she sounds distracted and there's a lot of background noise on her end.

"Hey, did I catch you at a bad time? It sounds like you're doing something."

"I'm just driving to the dance studio, but I have you on bluetooth," she explains. "How is the birthday girl?"

"My birthday was two days ago," I say with a laugh. "Remember the forty messages you sent me?"

"Oh, you loved them, don't lie."

I did love them, especially since I hadn't heard from her in four weeks before then. "I went to a bar last night, and I feel like garbage right now."

"Of course you did." I can't put a finger on her tone, but I can definitely tell she isn't laughing or smiling through the phone. "It looks like you've been partying it up out there," she comments.

I shrug my shoulders as if she can see me. "Well, yeah, we're not on tour anymore," I explain.

"Right, how is it being off tour?"

"It's weird," I laugh. "At first when I was on tour, I was so nervous and homesick. It felt like so many things were coming at me at once and it was just *so* overwhelming. Now that I'm not on tour though, it feels like I'm just sitting around and twiddling my thumbs."

I can hear her signal for a lane change. "Hard life."

An exasperated sigh leaves my lips. "OK, what's wrong?"

She shuts her car off as she says, "It's just that you're complaining about a life that you've always wanted. Giovanna, I know that your new life would take a while to get used to, but you have to understand that I'm still here living the same life I've always lived. To hear you complain about all the glory that you've gained, it's annoying, if I'm being completely honest."

She's always been honest, and I've always admired her for it, but this is a blow that I wasn't prepared for. I called my best friend with the intention of having someone to talk to, since I'm frustrated with the boys right now and I haven't made a true friend in Hollywood, so I thought calling Mary would be a good idea. I can see where she is coming from, of course, but that's a response I expected to get from the press. I thought my best friend would understand where I'm coming from like she always has in the past.

"I'll let you go then," I whisper through the lump in my throat. I can feel my heart sink to the bottom of my stomach as I hang up before she can even respond.

Being on tour was overwhelming, how can she not understand that? I would see hundreds and thousands of comments on our YouTube channel about how excited fans were for the album to drop, and that should have made me excited. It only partially did, though. It made me sick to my stomach because I was worried that the album we would produce would not live up to the expectations people had. I found myself stuck in this rut of *what if, what if, what if.* There would be days at a time where I would just stop writing songs completely because I was so unhappy with what I was coming up with, and this has become a process that I seem to repeat every time it's time for a new album.

It's getting better though, because as time passes, the more I learn. I know what I excel at and what I don't, but that doesn't mean I can write whatever I want. I'm still under strict commandment from Reen, and I wish I had a lot more freedom then I do. The work is still mine, but it has to be approved to the point where I'm scared to bring raw, emotional songs to them because they will throw the paper back at me. I just thought that Mary would be understanding, but she couldn't have sounded more uninterested and bothered.

I don't care for many people in the singing industry, I find them shallow and ignorant, so I don't consider anyone out there someone I would go on a coffee date with. I was hoping that Mary and I could stay as close as we were even though I've moved out here, but that's obviously not possible.

I scrunch my face right as Luca walks into my room. "Oh my gosh!" I yelp, placing my hand on my chest in hopes to bring down my heart rate.

"What?" he asks casually as if he barges into everyone's room.

"Ever heard of knocking?" I don't know why I feel the need to cross my arms, but I do.

"*Amore*, I think we're past the knocking stage."

I blush. I scoff after, because if only the paparazzi could see me now. Giovanni Rossi, painted as "the most confident woman out there", blushing at her boyfriend.

This is what Luca Fonzo does to me.

I roll my eyes. "Luca, stop it," I say.

He sits down on the corner of my bed and opens his arms, inviting me to sit next to him. I can't resist. "I'm sorry, there was a better way to say what I meant back there."

I huff. "Luca, I swear, if I had a dollar for everytime you say 'that's not what I said, but that's what I meant', I would be filthy rich."

He smiles at me and I smile back at the irony of what I just said. "Well, figuratively speaking," I clarify.

Luca continues, not letting the eye contact break. "I'm not good at writing songs, but if you ever need help choosing what lines to keep or what to write about, I can give you my opinion. Only if you want."

"I would love that."

"I'm sure Samantha and everyone will like whatever you give them," he reassures me. "There's no need to worry."

I shrug. "I'm starting to write outside of my comfort zone and I don't know how they will react."

"The fans will like anything you give them."

"I'm talking about my family. Our families."

He zones out, thinking about what I just said. "I never thought about that."

"I mean, I'm sure they're not blind," I babble on. "They obviously see all the pictures of us that get posted every five seconds."

"Gia, we've been to the bar *once*," he reminds me.

"But still."

"Well then?"

"That's just the start of it, though, what if-"

He laughs. "Gia, you and I both know that we will be at the club every night until the ugly lights come on, and here is a newsflash: they did the same thing when they were younger."

I look at him with big eyes. "Do they have to know the exact details, though?"

Luca cups my face in his soft hands. "You, my dear Gia, need to learn to say 'fuck it'."

I gush, breaking eye contact. "Look at how far you've come," he continues. "You've had to do whatever you've had to do to get right here, and now you're going to hold yourself back? I'm sorry, but I will not stand by and watch you do that to yourself. You are Giovanna Rossi, and it's time to show the world that you can have a good time just like everyone else."

I get up, pace for a bit, and then sit back down without saying a word. That's one of the things I love about our relationship: we've learned to let the silence stretch out between us whenever it is necessary for us to think it out.

"Alright." I grab his hand and smile. "Fuck it."

I kick Luca out as nicely as possible and grab my songbook.

I write five songs in one sitting.

Chapter 21

I COULD SIT FOR hours on the tour bus, but take-offs? I completely lose it.

"Gia, your knuckles are turning white," Tony points out, furrowing his brow with concern.

"I'm fine," I say with no reassurance at all. "You know how I feel about take-offs."

Luca unlatches my fingers from the arm rest and holds my hand. "It's fine, we've done this flight before, remember? Everything is going to be fine."

I nod my head, tightening my grip on his hand. "Right."

The three of us snap our heads up at the sound of two girls gasping. By the sounds of it, you would think they had just seen a ghost or a horrific accident took place right before their eyes.

No. They saw us.

"You're Insieme!" One of the girls with wavy red hair runs up to us, pointing her finger.

I shrug. "I've never heard of them." She takes a step back, unsure of how to react, so I give her a kind smile. "I'm only messing with ya."

That line never fails to confuse people; I love using it.

Her and her friend, who looks like she could be her sister, breathe out a sigh of relief and immediately pull out their phones. "Could we get a picture?"

Please. None of the fans ever say 'please'. They are already turning around and holding their phone up before we even say it is okay.

To be honest, I don't even want my picture taken because I look like death rolled over. Tony wanted to take a private jet that Reen offered, but I didn't even want to get first class seats because I think it is a waste of money that could go towards more necessary things. Like flights for our families or charities.

Now I wish I had listened to him, but I would never let my fans see that.

The three of us put on our Hollywood smile, making sure to angle our heads right so our faces don't look lopsided or we have a double chin.

"We are huge fans!" The other girl says once the picture is taken.

"Thank you," Tony says.

"Could you sign my hand?" She is already shoving her balled wrist and pen towards Luca, who clearly looks uncomfortable.

There are worse things to sign, I think, so I give his knee a gentle squeeze. I silently pray for the seatbelt light to flick on, but that does not happen.

Luca scribbles his initials and gives a weak nod. "Looks like you two should find your seats." He's trying to be as polite as possible, and to anyone else it sounds like he's the sweetest man ever, but Tony and I can hear that he's a little grumpy.

"Oh. My. Gosh. He is just so cute," one of them whispers to the other, but intentionally loud enough for us to hear. Luca puts his arm around me and I instinctively lean into him.

"It was really nice meeting you guys."

I smile at them. "Take care."

They leave, squealing up and down the aisle. I turn to Tony so fast that I almost get whiplash. "I'll take you up on that private jet offer."

He chuckles and shrugs his shoulders. "At least we can all agree that I'm always right."

I roll my eyes. "I didn't even want my picture taken! I mean, look at me!" I point down to Luca's sweatpants that are five sizes too big for me and my brother's hoodie I stole from him years ago.

"It's fine, people can't expect you to be in dresses and skirts all the time."

"I guess. You never know with the press, though."

"But next time listen to me."

"Okay."

Luca lets out an exasperated sigh. "Oh, boy."

The three of us hang our heads once we see the mob of people rushing towards our seats. You would think that the staff would urge people to take their seats, especially since the seatbelt light has just gone on, but that is not the case. The staff is trying to get a picture with us too.

I can't breathe.

So many pieces of paper are being thrown in my face and people are yelling at me to sign it. I can hear their cameras go off, even though I'm not even looking at the camera. *What if I look ugly?*

I need to get out of here, but there's nowhere to go. No escape.

So I sit there. I sign papers, crumpled up gum wrappers, and the odd hand. I put on a fake smile, if only to hide the tears swelling up in my chest.

I just want to go home and see my family. I want to go back home and just be Gia. I should be allowed to wear my sweatpants and look disheveled without cameras flashing.

"Let her breathe!" Luca has to yell over the crowd, but they show no signs of backing off. If anything, they push forward even more; I'm convinced the seats in front of us are going to snap any minute.

"That's enough." My voice is weak, even though I spoke as loud as I possibly could, but they drowned me out. I miss my security guards and I'm kicking myself for declining everything Reen offered for us on this trip. Since we are going home, I didn't want my family to see all the private jets and the security guards, but oh how I wish I could have just gotten over myself.

"That's it!" Tony unbuckles his seatbelt and stands up. The fans seem to be scared of Tony (for whatever reason, I would be more scared of Luca if I was them), and they back off slowly.

Too slowly for my liking, but they end up leaving nonetheless.

"Finally," I whisper so low that only the boys can hear me.

"I was right," Tony says, but he's not being boastful this time. If anything, he sounds shocked at how much more attention we've been getting recently.

I shrug my shoulders. "It's kind of just common sense, no? Like do they think we want to take pictures when we just rolled out of bed? I'm sure they wouldn't want a thousand cameras shoved into their faces as soon as they step onto an airplane…"

I'm pretty sure the boys tune me out, because I go on and on forever. They never stop me, they let me speak until I don't even realize that the take off is over and we are soaring high over the clouds.

I finally shut my mouth and turn to Luca because Tony is already snoring. "Would you mind flagging down the lady when she comes by with the drinks, please?"

He leans his head on mine. "Of course."

I flutter my eyes shut and match my breathing with Luca's. "I'm so excited to see everyone."

Luca shifts slightly, raising his hand just like I asked him to. Within seconds, the worker is in our aisle asking what we will have. "I'll have a glass of wine, please," I say as sweetly as I possibly can.

She nods her head. "Of course, ma'am, and would you like red or white?"

"Red, if you have it, please."

"We have anything you need." She pours the wine into a plastic cup and asks if she could get Luca anything. Luca orders a glass of wine as well, and I gently tap Tony on the leg.

"Are we there?" Tony sits up way too quickly.

I shake my head. "No, would you like anything?"

He orders what we all have, even though I know he prefers white wine, but Tony, surprisingly, has never been the complicated one when it comes to others. I've always admired that about him, how he wants to make people's lives as easy as possible.

The lady leaves us after she asked fifty times if there was anything else we need, and I raise my glass.

"Here's to us. For everything we've done for ourselves."

"To us," They say back.

As the sweet wine goes down my throat and I finish the glass in about three sips, a wave of tiredness washes over me.

I fell asleep on Luca with a smile on my face. Yes, being swarmed first thing in the morning isn't ideal, but it will be worth it. We are finally going home again.

Chapter 22

OUR BAGS WERE DELAYED, meaning that even more people wanted pictures with us because we couldn't get out of the airport. Despite all the hoodies and sunglasses we wear, everyone recognizes us.

Make no mistake, I am so thankful for the life I live and I recognize the fact that the fans asking for pictures right now are the ones who allow Insieme to even be a thing. But can you understand how frustrating it is to know that your baggage has been delayed and you haven't seen your family in a year, and now you have to stay in the airport with hundreds of people coming up to you from left right and center?

The belt hasn't moved in thirty minutes, but slowly, the bags start to appear. I say goodbye to the fans and practically dash out once I get my hands on my boring black suitcase with Tony and Luca following closely on my heels.

I flag down a taxi and put on my sunglasses. I didn't realize it would be this sunny, but I love any excuse to wear my Dior sunglasses.

Ever since I treated myself to these big, pink-lense sunglasses that practically cover my whole face, I basically live in them.

"You're taking this whole '70's thing a bit far," Tony teases.

"Oh, don't pretend like you don't compliment my outfits everyday."

Lately, I've been trying to dress more flamboyantly for the press. "You're in sweatpants," he points out.

"Yes, it's a change from my wild dresses and gold hoop earrings, but I still love these sunglasses, and you do too."

He shrugs his shoulders. "You change personalities and styles like every year."

Luca laughs. "This look will be gone in a few months."

I scoff at their stupidity. "Have you read any articles lately? Teenage girls around the world are shoving each other out of the way so they can purchase a pair of gold earrings."

"They've become your signature, sure," Luca responds, "but you're not wearing them right now."

I roll my eyes. "Am I supposed to wear those clogs on my ears during a flight?"

Tony opens the taxi door and we all squeeze into the backseat of the cab, and of course I'm in the middle. "I wouldn't be surprised if there is an article saying they are concerned for you."

"What address?" The taxi driver says.

"How's it going, sir?" Luca asks. He's always so concerned about how everyone is doing, and I love him for it.

"Good. Address?"

I tell him my address because it would be easiest to drop me off first since the boys are still neighbors.

Luca clears his throat and sits up. "My mom was wondering if you guys would like to come over for dinner."

I can't hide my smirk, I just know it was Giancarlo's idea. "I'd love that."

Tony opens his phone dramatically, looking at his calendar. "What time are we thinking? I'm pretty busy."

The three of us let out an obnoxious laugh that makes the driver shoot his eyebrows up and form a scowl on his lips.

"Can I bring anything?" I offer. "Dessert?"

Luca shakes his head. "Remember what Samantha has been saying?"

Oh. That's right, I forgot. Samantha wants us on a strict diet because of the popularity we have been gaining- at least, that's her reasoning behind stopping me from ordering a hamburger now.

"I miss my hamburgers," I pout, folding my arms over my chest and jutting out my lip. I am well aware that I sound like a baby, but I don't care.

Samantha, well and Reen in general, are saying that we will be doing even more concerts. They're already looking into portable equipment so we could possibly record songs on the tour buses in

between cities. Because we will be doing more
shows, it is important for us to maintain a healthy
lifestyle. We don't want to be out of breath on stage.

I don't think there is any harm in a
hamburger once in a while, but Reen doesn't agree.

"I know, but we have to stick to the diet,"
Luca says softly. I know he isn't keen on the idea
either, but he's always been the one to follow the
rules.

I sigh, "You do realize we break our diet
every night when we drink our calories."

He gives me a deep smile and chuckles at
his response before he even says it. "It's different
because you're drinking and dancing it off
simultaneously, so it all works out in the end."

"Right…" I coax my eyebrow up, not at all
convinced.

"But seriously, Luca, if you need us to bring
anything, just let us know," Tony says.

"Of course."

The driver, going twenty over the speed limit, gets me to my home in no time. I am stuck to my seat as I look at my home.

Nothing has changed.

I don't know why, but tears start to roll down my cheeks. I promised myself I would keep it together for my family, yet here I am.

Luca gets out of the car and holds the door open for me and I say goodbye to them. Tony makes some comment about making sure I'm dressed for the occasion, but I don't even care enough to shoot a response back at him.

The taxi tires screech against the road as the boys head off towards their families. I take a few deep breaths, the wine from the flight has gone straight to my head.

"No way."

I know my brother's voice from a mile away, and I just knew he wouldn't even give me a chance to ring the doorbell.

"Is that my, *fratello*?" I choke on my tears, but he doesn't seem to notice and embraces me in a hug.

"My *sorella*, I've missed you so much."

I don't think I'll ever get used to being away from them for so long. Ever.

"Let's go inside," he urges, taking my suitcase from me. Calmness washes over me as I realize that everything is nearly in the exact same spot as when I left. It's funny how things never change in this home. It looks like I still live here.

I'm greeted with an even warmer welcome from my mom and dad, and all four of us are crying. I'm glad I'm not the only emotional one.

"It's so good to be back," I say, sitting on the couch and reclining. I used to sit on this very couch years ago and watch Insieme's first YouTube videos, all the memories rushing back to me.

"We miss you, but we wouldn't change anything," my dad says. "You make us so proud."

My little heart bursts with joy inside my chest. "That's all I've ever wanted," I whisper.

My mother smiles at me. "I've always known you would make it in the industry, remember when I told you that?"

"I do." They've always been my number one fan- my number one *supporter*- and I cannot express my gratitude enough.

We spend about three hours just catching up and I tell them all about what it's like living in Los Angeles. When I talk, they listen with such attention that it's actually a tad intimidating. Occasionally, my dad will shoot me a skeptical look, but I reassure him that I'm being safe and everything is great out there. I tell them that the boys are there to stop me from doing stupid shit.

"I don't know if you guys know, but we've been invited to Luca's house tonight for dinner," I share.

"We should get ready then," my mother declares.

"It's going to be so nice," I say. "It's just going to be like old times."

"Except you guys have millions of dollars and even more fans," my brother comments. There isn't a hint of jealousy in his voice, and I love him for it. He's been making a great life for himself, just like I always knew he would.

You see, here's the thing: every member of the Rossi family knows that we will be just fine. And if one of us needs that extra push to get out of our own way, the other is there to give them the nudge. We are a family, always have been and always will be.

And even though we are living our separate lives- me with my career, my brother with his job, and my parents still running a business- we will always be there for eachother.

So as I get up and think about what I'm wearing to dinner, I can't help but smile. My family has always been my rock, even when I moved out.

But I realize that what Insieme is, what the boys and I have, that's a family bond that cannot and will not be broken. Insieme can only go up from here, and we will get each other through the next busy period of our careers because that is simply what family does.

Chapter 23

"THIS IS A NICE SURPRISE."

"Shut up, Gia," Luca laughs.

Giancarlo shoots me a smile. "Some things never change." I can tell he wants me to elaborate more on the issue, seeing as though the last time he was over I was having a meltdown, but he doesn't push any further.

"Be nice, Gia," my mother chids.

We sit down, and of course, like the great Italians we are, Anna has a plate of piping hot pasta bowls infront of us.

Tony nudges Luca with his elbow. "I think they're going to love their gift."

"What gift?" Lorenzo says, taking his seat next to me. He's grown even more, and yes, he is taller than me- almost everyone is. I never take off the bracelet he got me, even more so now because gold jewelry is now my signature.

Luca tilts his head back and sighs. "You have to stop spoiling our surprises, T."

Tony lifts his shoulders up and down. "It's not like they didn't know it was coming."

"You didn't have to get us anything," Anna says as she takes her spot and says *bon appetit*, allowing everyone to dig in.

The burst of fresh tomato sauce melts on my tongue and I have to stop myself from drooling. It's such a nice treat after only being on salads and protein shakes.

"This is amazing, Anna," I comment.

"Yeah, it's great, Mom." The silence stretches across the room as soon as Vince opens his mouth.

The Fonzo brothers are still divided, that hasn't changed. Insieme has grown a huge amount in just over a year compared to where we were when we first started out. Insieme has grown, but Luca and Vince's relationship has not.

I can't sugar coat it, it's nice to sit at this table knowing that we proved Vince wrong. We made it. I know we've made it everytime we step foot outside of our house and everyone goes crazy. I know we've made it everytime I step foot on any stage and fans scream so loud that it pierces through my brain.

My dad clears his throat. "Do you know how long you're staying here?"

"A week," I answer.

"That's nice," my brother says.

"You think so?" Vince asks, refusing to look at the boys and I and keeps his gaze on Antonio. "Because I think it's bullshit that they can only take a week's holiday."

Luca and Lorenzo tense on either side of me, and Luca looks at me as he responds to his older brother. "Well, we have to get back in time to start writing and recording our new album."

Tony pipes in, again, looking at me so they don't have to talk to Vince directly. "It's going to be a lot of work when we get back."

I nod my head, staring down Vince, but he doesn't dare meet my fiery gaze. "Millions of people are waiting for our new album to drop, so it's all hands on deck."

Vince sits back in his chair, slouching as if he is bored. "Right."

I go back to eating my dinner, trying to enjoy this cheat day and this visit without Vince ruining it for me.

"Do you have a name for the album yet?" Lorenzo asks.

Luca shakes his head. "We haven't really talked about it."

"Better get to work then," Vince says sharply.

"That's enough," Anna scolds. Giancarlo flares out his nostrils, I can tell he's upset from the shaky breaths he's taking. Luca does the same thing when he's furious.

"I'll go get the gift," I say, if only to ease the obvious tension. Luca and Tony follow closely on my heels as we go upstairs to Luca's bedroom.

As soon as I step foot in his bedroom, memories of that night rush back to me. The first time Luca actually told me he loved me, and then he kissed me like no one has ever kissed me before, but I was with Danny. He was actually really rude that night, but he was just trying to cope. I can't blame him for being so upset. He was being open and vulnerable, and I was a closed vault not willing to open up to anyone.

Luca cracked me.

From the very first sleepover when we stayed up for hours I felt truly comfortable with him. I don't think I've ever laughed so much with someone, yet I tried to push away the undeniable chemistry.

Looking back, I was so stupid to try and fight my feelings for him off. Past relationships, the multiple heartbreaks I had faced, they all held me back. I would be lying if I told you I don't regret not jumping into this relationship sooner. I had to stop using my past as an excuse and let myself open up to Luca.

He was the best thing to ever happen to me. He showed me what real love is like, even at sixteen years of age.

"Gia, where are you right now?" Luca asks, snapping me out of my thoughts.

I smile and shake my head, dismissing the memories. Tony opens Luca's closet and pulls out three big gift bags. We got our families plaques of our albums so they can display it in their homes, I hope they like it.

I catch Luca's eyes while Tony's back is facing us. *I love you*, I mouth.

I love you too, he mouths back.

I let out a small laugh. "What?" Tony asks, spinning around.

"Nothing."

"I'm always missing shit between you two," he complains, putting the cards in their designated bags.

We head back downstairs and give our parents their gifts.

"It's too much," Susana insists with tears in her eyes.

"After letting me keep your *Purple Rain* shirt, I think this is the least I could do for you," I say. Susana tries to wipe her tears away quickly, but fails and lets her emotions get the best of her.

"Do you like it?" Tony asks.

"Please, Giovanna, that was nothing compared to this gift. Yes, I love it."

Tony lets out a sigh of relief. He is always telling Luca and I that we should not seek the approval of others and do whatever we want with our career. He is the biggest advocate for not checking our social media because he doesn't want us putting out work that isn't truly authentic because it's based on other's opinions. But if there's one thing he seeks, it's Susana's approval and validation.

We get up and give everyone hugs, emphasizing that the gift was the least we could have done for them.

The rest of the evening, we talk about absolutely nothing. It's nice to have a normal conversation because lately everything has been about this new album- what we can do better, what our new goals are, what audience we are trying to reach, the whole nine yards.

I am so grateful for Samantha and how she believed in us, but it's nice to talk to my family and not my manager every now and then.

"We should head off," my mother says in between yawns.

My eyes are heavy, but I don't want this night to end. With every passing day, we get older, and I'm afraid that nights where all our families are together and going to become more and more limited.

"Thanks for having us," I say, getting up to give everyone a hug. Lorenzo hugs me extra tight, and I don't even nod at Vince.

"You guys aren't going out?" Antonio asks.

"Oh, I meant the three of us should head out, you can go out if you want," Mom clarifies.

She's getting more relaxed with age. I guess your daughter moving out at such a young age does something to you.

I look at the boys and they are looking at me with big eyes and nodding their heads. "It's late, I don't think anything is open anyway."

I would love to go out, but what kind of daughter would I be if I just let my family go to bed without me being home? Besides, I literally live with the boys, I'm sure we can spend *one* night away from each other.

"I'm sure we can find a 24/7 diner," Tony suggests, almost pleading. He has attachment issues, and it's actually really cute that he wants to spend so much time with me.

I shake my head and move towards the door. "I should get a good night's sleep." His shoulders deflate. "But maybe tomorrow." Tony smiles again and he gives me a hug.

"Goodnight, Gia," Tony says, hugging me tighter.

"Okay, T, it's just one night," I laugh, but stop when I look up and his vision is no longer focused and his lips are in a thin line.

"We've been living with each other for years, it's going to be difficult for me to wake up and have nobody to take pictures of."

"What pictures?" Lorenzo, sweet Lorenzo, asks.

"Nothing," I blurt.

"These ones." Tony pulls out his phone within seconds and shows me snuggled up to Luca on the couch with my mouth hanging open and drool pooling on Luca's gray sweatshirt.

My cheeks burn like flames and my neck hairs shoot up. I love Luca, I really do, but in front of my parents? That's just embarrassing for them to see.

"How do you think I feel," Luca says, jutting out his lip sarcastically.

"Exactly! This is why we should spend the night together like we have for the last two years," Tony reasons.

Luca slaps his hand to his face and cracks a smile. "T, I was kidding, let the poor girl go home."

"Fine."

"Why are you clenching your jaw?" Susana asks her son.

"Is it such a crime to want to spend everyday with my best friends?"

"How about I call you when I get home?" I suggest. I know Tony doesn't want me to feel guilty for turning him down, but now I feel bad. Although moving in with the boys has been the best and I wouldn't trade it for anything, it will be kind of nice to have just one night to myself.

I feed off of other people's energy, but I also find comfort in being alone. I will never apologize for that. I don't think I, or anyone else, should feel bad for that.

"Deal."

"Goodnight, *amore*," Luca whispers, giving me a hug and kissing me subtly on my cheek.

"Bye, everyone!"

I can barely keep my eyes open the whole car ride home, and now that I'm staring at my phone in my bed, I wish I could shut off my brain.

Don't do it. Don't do it. Please, don't do it.

I do it anyway. I search up my name on Google and thousands of photos and articles pop up. I scoff louder than intended and forward a link to Tony and write him a message.

Me: You were right. Goodnight, T.

I throw my phone on the ground and grab my teddy bear. Some people really do have too much time on their hands, but at least they make my life entertaining.

I don't care how dumb, mean, or irrelivant an article is about me, it attracts more fans; I have to remember that.

My breathing starts to become more steady and slower as I think about my life and how the people I was with tonight know the real me. Family comes first.

I fall asleep with a smile on my face, knowing that I will always have a safety net to catch me through all the bullshit my career throws my way.

Breaking News

Entertainment Tonight!

That's right, folks, take a good look at that picture. Is it possible that the sensational singer, Giovanna Rossi, is calling it quits? Today, Rossi was spotted at the airport going home to "visit family", but is that really the case? It seems she's ditched her gold jewelry, and her outfit choice... let's just say that she's seen better days.

She was spotted with other band members, Luca Fonzo and Tony Chiati, but we can't help but wonder if this could be the end of Insieme. They seem to be in rough shape after their first tour. Who knows, maybe a couple of kids weren't prepared for Hollywood?

Chapter 24

"ARE YOU SERIOUS?" LUCA almost throws his phone across my family room, but thinks better of it and holds it in a death grip instead.

"How stupid," Tony says.

I laugh and shake my head. "I guess this is good for the new album, though. People will expect us to stop making music, and then *BAM*! We will come out with our best album yet."

"How idiotic." Tony is in his own little world.

"That's actually a great point, *amore*," Luca comments, both of us choosing to let Tony do his own thing.

"We just have to work extra hard to get this album released then." I can already feel the pressure building onto my chest as I say that.

"But, like, you just wore sweatpants one time," Tony huffs.

"I don't know why you're so upset, you're the one who called it," I point out.

"It was a joke!"

"But you were still right." Giving Tony shit is my favorite pastime.

"I didn't think it would actually get published!"

I shrug my shoulders. "Maybe people overhead you and they really took it to heart."

"How is this my fault?!"

"Just saying."

"*Amore*, don't gaslight him," Luca interjects.

"Seriously, though," I say, regaining my focus, "I think this is a prime opportunity."

Tony nods his head. "I would tell you it's a good idea, but you're being a little shit right now."

I flash him a smile. "I'm just messing with you."

Tony folds his arms and cocks his head to the side stubbornly. He makes a *hmph* sound in the back of his throat.

Luca sighs loudly. "If you're looking for her to apologize, you can stop holding your breath."

I make my mouth into an O and widen my eyes. "Okay, so I never apologize now?"

"Are you serious? I think I can count on one hand how many times you have apologized."

"There's no need for me to apologize."

"Let me guess, because you're perfect."

"Glad we're all on the same page."

"What am I going to do with this one?" Luca asks Tony with a slight laugh.

"You mean what am *I* going to do with *you*," I correct him.

Luca rolls his eyes. "Okay, we don't have time for this type of bickering."

"Yeah, being back home has made you act like a 16- year-old again," Tony adds.

At that, I genuinely roll my eyes. "You're the one who was just tapping your foot because you expected an apology!"

Luca stands up. "Okay, enough! Gia is right, we have to get this album recorded and done so people won't expect it."

"How fast are we thinking?" I ask, already panicking just thinking about how many songs I have to write.

"That's a question for our management," Tony answers. "I think we should try and get most of the songs written in about two weeks."

"Songs don't come to me just like that." I snap my fingers.

"We know, and we are ready to help you, remember our conversation?"

"Right."

"Right."

"Okay, then."

"Sounds good," Luca says, clapping his hands together and rubbing them excitedly.

"I guess I should get to work then," I say, getting off of the couch. "I'll be right back." I head upstairs to my bedroom, grab my song book, and run back to the boys.

"So I already have five songs written, if you guys want to take a look." My mouth is going faster than both my hands and my brain.

Luca takes my book and Tony hovers over him to inspect my work. I don't think this nervous feeling that starts at the tip of my toes and goes all the way to my head will ever go away. I love the boys, we are close, but they are still reading my thoughts and I feel quite vulnerable.

I have five songs written: "Another Late Night", "Other Side", "Whatever Happens, Happens", "Across the Floor", and "Is this Real?"

"What I'm thinking," I say as the boys keep reading because I just can't stop talking when I'm nervous, "is that we talk about a love story." The boys shoot me a slight frown, so I quickly explain. "Think about this: at the start of the album, it's about people walking into the club just looking for another late night of parties. For the first couple of songs, they are just out to have fun and they don't really care what happens.

"However, towards the middle of the album, I'm thinking around song five, they meet someone. They catch the love of their life's eye across the dance floor, and the rest of the album turns out to be their love story and how they help each other develop and mature."

The boys are silent. Irritably silent. And they're still silent.

More silence.

<small>Silence.</small>

"Somebody say something," I blurt. "I can't handle this awkwardness."

Luca leans forward to place my song book- my deepest thoughts and emotions- down onto the coffee table and leans back onto the couch. Tony leans back as well, the both of them clearing their throat.

"Hello?"

I'm going to punch them in the face.

"I... Gia, I love it," Luca whispers.

"You little piece of..."

Tony jumps up and shakes my shoulders with a big smile on his face. "That's payback for gaslighting me!"

I laugh, my cheeks going a rosey red. "Okay, okay, I deserve it."

"No way you just admitted-"

"I guess," I say, flashing Luca a smile.

"Okay, but seriously, I love that idea," Tony announces.

"Anything I should change?" I ask.

They both shake their heads. "I think you should roll with it," Luca encourages.

"How did you come up with this?" Tony asks.

I place my hand on my hip and shift my weight. "I know, it's hard being this talented." I'm not even joking when I say it. I mean, it's brilliant if you ask me.

"I hate you," Tony scoffs.

"I thought this would be a good balance between what I typically write and what Reen is looking for," I explain, choosing to ignore Tony's words because we all saw him nearly breakdown last night when he found out we wouldn't be spending the night together.

Luca's eyes go wide. "A balance between love and partying."

I clap my hands and point to him. "Exactly!"

"You're a genius, *amore*."

"Stop." I flick my wrist down and put my left cheek to my left shoulder. "It goes straight to my ego."

"This is great, this is really great," Tony says. "So we should probably write a couple more songs before going out tonight."

"I'm really not in the mood to go out," Luca sighs.

"But we didn't go out last night," I mention.

"We don't have to go out every night," he shoots back.

"But how do you expect us to write a great album if we don't experience it for ourselves."

"And you mean to tell me that you don't have enough experience already." Luca springs his eyebrows up, not at all convinced.

"Something new could happen tonight," I counter.

"That's true," Tony backs me up.

Luca shakes his head, knowing that this battle is already lost. "Fine, but remember that there are plenty of clubs back in LA; this trip is for spending time with family."

"Yes, of course, but our families go to bed at like 8 o'clock."

"Just making that clear," Luca says.

I pick up my songbook and motion for the boys to leave. "I agree, Luca, so you guys should get going and spend as much time with your families."

"See you tonight," Luca says, heading for the door already after giving me a gentle hug.

"One last thing, Gia," Tony beams.

"What's up?"

"Be prepared for the best party years of our lives."

Chapter 25

I FOLLOW FIVE SIMPLE steps on our trip:

Step #1: Wake up before the sun rises so I can write a couple songs.

Step #2: Convenience our parents to go out every hour of every day.

Step #3: Have family dinners, and then all meet up and catch a taxi to the latest and greatest club.

Step #4: Lose count of the drinks we've had, stumble into the back of a cab, somehow end up at home.

Step #5: Repeat.

That's pretty much it, and it's been the best trip of my life. I couldn't even tell you if people were snapping pictures of me, mostly because I don't really remember events that occur the night before when I wake up. But I can tell you that being back home was the cleanse that I needed.

Now that I'm in town, I asked Mary to meet for coffee, even though we both know I will order anything but coffee. After our last conversation, I'm a little bit nervous sitting across from her now, but I hope she can't tell. At the end of the day, she's my best friend and maybe she was just having an off day, so I decided before I got here not to get into an argument over something as small as her tone.

"I'm glad to be back," I say, taking a sip from my tea. "I really missed it."

"It's always good to hear from you." She drinks her coffee and clears her throat. "So tell me something new. I feel like I never hear from you these days!"

She says it with a smile, but my stomach drops. Does she feel like I'm ignoring her? That's not what I intended for, life just got really busy. "I've been swamped with work," I explain.

"It is a difficult job you have. Touring the world, selling out stadiums, I get it."

I pinch a tight smile out. I told myself I wouldn't get into an argument, so I decide to act like everything is normal. "We're actually set to go on tour pretty quickly here."

"That's exciting," she says, swallowing her coffee.

"Hey! You should come to one of the European shows!" I genuinely suggest it. "I would love to have you there."

"If I can get the time off of work then I will definitely try and make it out there. I can't make any promises though."

"Yeah, of course," I say, trying to hide my disappointment. I can tell by her tone that she will not be making it out there. I mean, what did I expect? She's grown just as much as I have. We're no longer some kids without jobs who can just get in a car and hang out now. So much has changed over the years, and I knew that as soon as Samantha made that first phone call to me that nothing would be the same. I guess I just thought that my friendship with Mary would be the only thing that stayed solid in my life.

We made small talk for the rest of the visit, but I was just trying to hide my disappointment the whole time. What I got from this reunion was that we're no longer best friends anymore. Maybe we just need some time apart, or maybe I just need to focus on my career, I don't know. The only thing I do know is this: I need a drink because I'm mourning the relationship I once had with Mary.

I know I'm good at my job. I have to believe that to be in this industry. We have been trying to prove ourselves for so long, simply because we still feel like we lucked out and we want to prove to people that we earned our spot in this business.

It's been go-go-go for nearly three years, it's been three years of seeking approval. Knowing that I'm good hasn't always been enough, it can only take me so far. But coming back here and sitting across from my brother in this small pizza joint and hearing him talk about how much of a genius he thinks I am, well… It's amazing.

Validation from people you've looked up to your whole life changes the way you see yourself. And it's exactly what I need right now, especially after this morning.

"I don't know how to describe it," Antonio states, "it's like I'm watching this goddess move across the stage."

I take another bite of my greasy pizza and hold a napkin to my lips. "Thank you," I say between bites.

"The lyrics are so, what's the word I'm looking for?" He puts his hand to his chin, searching for the right word. "Complex."

"Is that good or bad?"

"It's *majestic*."

I can't help the obnoxious laugh that escapes past my lips. "You're making me gush."

"I'm serious, Gia, you came up with a hit when you were 16! That's amazing, and I can't tell you how proud I am of you."

I put my head down, not wanting to look into his eyes, knowing I will break into tears if I do. That's all I've ever wanted to hear. "You really wanted me to go and pursue this." I thought I would never be able to just up and leave my family, but it was Antonio who urged me to go and not pass up on a golden opportunity.

"I always knew you were different."

"I always needed you to give me that extra push."

"That's what bestfriends are for."

I look up, already finding him smiling back at me. I'm so grateful my brother and I have always been close and we have been able to understand each other on a level that no one else can. No one and no amount of time can take that bond away.

"So besides making amazing songs, how have you been?" he asks. "How are things going between you and Luca?"

I put down my slice of pizza and suck my teeth. "He's amazing. Wait, do you want me to go into all that lovey-dovey stuff?"

"Please do." He motions his hands for me to continue.

I bury my face in my hands. I've been dying to tell someone I trust about how things are going. "I love him a lot. He has this effect on me that I don't even understand. And that's okay because I don't need to understand every little thing, I just know that it's right."

"Can you see yourself getting serious with him?"

I stop in my tracks. "Aren't we already serious?"

"Yeah, but dating and marriage are completely different things," he says matter-of-factly. With anyone else, I would be totally uncomfortable talking about this, but not with Antonio.

"I mean, we have been together for years now, but I haven't really considered marriage because we are still so young."

"Interesting." He offers nothing less and nothing more.

I continue on my train of thought. "You've seen all the pictures, there are thousands of people coming to our concerts, but I only see him. When we share a microphone and harmonize, it's like everything disappears."

Antonio fakes a gag and rolls his eyes. "Okay, too lovey-dovey, *sorella*."

I shrug my shoulders. "I really do love him."

But can I see myself marrying him? I don't know. I don't even know what's going to happen tomorrow, how can I predict if Luca and I are going to get married?

"Look, Gia, I am really happy for you. Please, don't think that I'm not. I see the way he looks at you, and let me tell you that he is head over heels for you. I know that he would literally die for you, there is no denying that. But you guys have been in a relationship for a while, have you guys even talked about getting engaged?"

"Honestly, we haven't. We moved out, we have been busting our asses to make this kind of lifestyle possible, so that discussion has not come up." It comes out harsher than I intended it to, so I try to smooth it out. "But now that our career is stable, I think it is important to consider our relationship's future."

Antonio nods his head. "I just don't want you to become too dependent on him."

"Of course," I say too quickly.

"You love him, he loves you, but you have to be strong enough on your own as well." I shoot my eyes down because I know that I'm not strong enough.

"Right. But I also think that the two of us together is better than the two of us apart," I counter.

"I'm not disputing that." He puts his hands up in surrender. "I just wanted to make sure that you guys are okay. Clearly, you are more than okay."

I smile at the ground. "He's perfect," I whisper. I truly mean it.

"I'm so glad you're happy."

"But anyways," I say, embarrassed that this has all been about me. "How have you been doing?"

"Fantastic," he states.

He tells me all about his new job, how he has his own apartment, how he's in a serious relationship, and how much he misses me. He talks for an hour straight, and I listen without, surprisingly, opening my mouth once.

"That's great, I'm glad to hear that everything is going good," I say.

"Look at us, all grown-up."

I give him a small laugh. "I'm still sixteen if you ask me."

Antonio makes his eyes go big. "Yeah, I've seen so many pictures."

"You guys should come down there more often now, so then maybe you can come join us," I suggest. My heart races, I am not able to take another decline to my offer, it will crush me.

"I'd love that," he says. I let out a small sigh of relief and smile at my brother.

The waitress places the bill down on the table and I quickly pick it up and pay for everything. "I'm really sad that I'm leaving tomorrow."

"You don't have to pay for me," he insists.

I hold up my hand. "It's the least I can do." I hand back the bill and thank the waitress, making sure to give her a good tip. She did ask for a picture as soon as she came up, but she was super nice.

"As selfish as it is, we don't want you to leave again," my brother says.

I shake my head. "I don't want to go back, either."

But I *do*. To be honest, I'm itching to get this new album out; I want to grow our fanbase. I'm so excited to get to work, because you know what? Bring on the fans.

I have a love-hate relationship with Insieme's fans, let's just make that clear. I *love* people looking up to me and waiting for us to drop new music, but I *hate* not being able to do normal things without getting room to breathe. It's really more of the paparazzi than the fans, but it's hard to decipher which one is which in the heat of the moment.

I just do not have the heart to tell my brother that I'm excited to head back to Los Angeles. Being away from all of it made me realize how comfortable I've actually become there.

"I know you're going to be super busy when you get back, but try and call us when you can; we love hearing from you," he says, getting out of his seat and putting his jacket on.

I mirror his actions and we walk out the door. "I'll call you everyday," I promise.

"Everyone knows you don't break a promise." I hear him let out a sigh of relief, and this makes me smile.

As we walk down the sidewalk without a particular destination in mind, I realize how much everything has changed, but yet nothing has changed at all. My brother and I are still best friends, even though we're older. My family still has all my teddy bears in my room. I still keep in touch with a select group of people from high school, because, really, who has more than five friends they keep in touch with after high school?

Everything has changed, yet this is still my home. I'll get on that plane tomorrow and head back to where we've settled, I'll sleep in a room next to Tony's with walls so thin that I can hear him snoring every night, I'll get up and go to a studio, and I'll go back and work for Reen- a managment company, for crying out loud.

But.

This.

Is.

My.

Home.

Chapter 26

AS SOON AS WE get back to Los Angeles, people are swarming us. The paparazzi is asking us questions about personal shit and it's grinding my gears.

But we eventually make it back to our house in one piece, though Tony is making a scene, but what's new?

"It's like, yeah, I know I'm the best and you want to know everything about me, but like back off," he rambles. He's been going on this tangent for about thirty minutes now, and I'm certain that both Luca and myself have tuned him out. We give him a slight *hm* every now and then, but we just let him speak for the most part.

"Here's the thing: we have a deadline approaching for this new album," Luca says.

"Which is?" Tony asks.

"Three months exactly."

"That's it?" I blurt. "How come my favorite artists release an album every two years, but we only have three months?"

Luca clears his throat. "But, Gia, we knew about this album deadline a long time ago."

I pinch my lips together, pour myself a gin and tonic, and get my song book out. "Still." I know I sound like a ten year-old, but I don't care.

"We'll get it done," Tony says. "I'm sure we'll be able to meet the deadline."

"We at least have to show them what we have so far; they're looking to get out a couple singles before the album drops."

"How many?" I ask, flipping through pages and pages of my scribbled notes, trying to understand an idea I had written down in the middle of the night. My song book is filled with lots of scribbles, sticky notes, highlights, quotes, and of course, songs- some finished and released, some forgotten or rejected by management- but I love this book with my heart. I don't even care that the cover is severely bent with a chunk ready to fall off any minute, because it's a piece of me that I get to share with the world.

Luca shrugs. "At least one, obviously, but maybe two or three."

"Okay," I say and then a long pause stretches throughout the room as I try to find my favorite songs.

"Which one tickles your fancy?" Tony asks, plopping down next to me, stretching his arm out around my shoulders.

I lift mine up and down, close my book and prop my feet up on the coffee table with my hands behind my head. "It really isn't up to me, but I think we should release one of our upbeat ones so fans get something new and there will be even more anticipation for the album."

Luca laughs. "As if rumors about you and your gold earrings weren't enough to draw people to the album." He stares at me with such intensity, never breaking eye contact. I hold eye contact, suddenly forgetting how to breathe or talk. How can someone get better looking with age?

Gone are the awkward teenage years, and I'm welcoming his new manhood with open arms.

He's still the same old caring Luca, but he's taller, his bone structure is more defined, and he's just way more confident now. Most of the time I find myself admiring him, and I'm sure he notices, but I just don't understand how I got into a relationship with someone way out of my league.

I blink, bringing myself back to reality. "I still think it's a good tactic," I offer. "We can see what Samantha has to say."

"We're going to the studio this afternoon, so for now let's just relax." Tony gets up from the couch and grabs three glasses, already getting the mimosa maker out.

"I didn't realize this was a baby shower for middle-aged women," Luca scoffs, making his way over to help Tony.

Tony tilts his head to the side, making his eyes wide. "You don't have to have any if that's how you feel about my precious mimosas."

"A little dramatic," Luca mumbles.

Tony, with all his experience, whips up the mimosas in three minutes. I know I shouldn't mix, but I accept mine anyway and we clink glasses, and I nearly choke on my drink when I see Tony lifting his pinky in the air while he takes a sip.

"What?" he demands. "What's so funny?" I'm shaking from my head down to my toes, unable to contain myself.

"Why is your pinky like that?" I spit out.

Tony rolls his eyes and takes a dramatic, big gulp. "It's called class, something *you* obviously don't have."

"I have more class in my pinky toe than you have in your entire body."

"Really? That just came out of your mouth? You do realize that you order a burger and the bun ends up falling apart every time you take a bite into it. You curse like it's going out of style. And can we talk about your manspreading? And *you're* talking to *me* about being classy."

"Shut up, T."

"Okay, you two, let's all relax," Luca interjects. He turns on the TV and puts on *Goodfellas*, if only to shut us up. It does.

"I'm going to get some shut eye before heading to the studio," I announce after the movie, the alcohol suddenly sending a wave of dizziness and fatigue through my blood. I set down the glass and leave the boys to bicker amongst themselves (I think I hear them talking about football, but I don't really know anymore).

I shut the door behind me, not even bothering to change out of my yoga pants and T shirt, and fall straight on my stomach. I grip my teddy bear and let my eyes fall shut, because maybe if I sleep, this due date will get pushed back a bit.

Chapter 27

OF COURSE WHEN I woke up, it didn't get pushed back. Now that we're at the studio, fiddling around with different scales on the guitar and keys on the piano, the due date seems all the more daunting.

"What about a little *do- do- duuu*," I suggest, trying to make my thoughts come to life with my zero communication skills.

Luca nods his head excitedly, I'm sure he just gave himself whiplash. "Yeah! Like this!" He plays the exact guitar riff I was trying to explain.

I shoot up from the piano bench, banging my knee on the piano. "OW! My knee!"

"Are you okay?" Luca asks at the same time Tony bursts out laughing.

"I'm fine," I say quickly. "I think we can do something with this on the piano." I bang on the keys until I find the right melody. "What do you think?"

"Is standing up really necessary right now?" Tony asks, he can't seem to stop laughing. I shoot him a funny look, smirking so he knows I'm not genuinely upset with him.

"I love it," Luca says, playing his guitar riff at the same time as I play the piano.

"Okay, okay, this is really good. This is really good," I say over and over again. I'm so excited that this album is finally coming together. "Now we just need to add the driving beat with the drums."

Of course, Samantha walks in right as we're hitting our stride in this album, and to be honest, she could not have come in at a worse time. When the boys and I get in our groove, it takes a lot for us to stop. We make hit after hit, writing only what we feel like at the moment.

"So is this going to be like a Huey Lewis & The News mixed with Bryan Adams type of album?" she asks, placing her large iced coffee down on the table.

"A little bit of John Mellancamp too," I add. Yeah, I've been in the car with my dad one too many times.

"Perfect, that is exactly what we were looking for." She sounds genuinely impressed as she takes a big swig from her coffee. I don't think there's been a day where she's walked into the studio without her coffee.

"We have most of the album written; we can start recording today," Tony says eagerly.

Samantha nods her head and looks at the hundreds of papers scattered around the room. I can see her face twist with confusion, you don't realize how hard you're working until you take a break to see just how much of a mess you've made.

At least the music is great.

"It might be easier if you just heard the songs, they're really great," I explain. "It's kind of hard to get the effect by just looking at a sheet of paper."

"That would be great," she says with a smile. She's just as excited as we are, and that's exactly what we need. Yes, we don't always see eye to eye. Yes, I am undeniably jealous of her gorgeous features. Yes, she is always up my ass about deadlines. But she is still a hard-core advocate for Insieme, and that makes me so happy that she saw our talent and believed in us and saw this relationship through. And she loves our songs.

We spend the next four hours recording, adding onto songs that we feel need more guitar or extra vocal parts. I can see the look on Samantha's face as I sing, and I just know that we hit a home run.

In between songs I take a few sips of whatever bottle I brought with me, and the best part is, the boys don't even question it. While they don't take part in my afternoon drinking, they don't bother to question me because they can see just how much better my ideas flow when I have it.

I'm severely dehydrated, covered in sweat, and way too jacked up on adrenaline by the end of the recording session. I'm bouncing off the walls as I walk over to Samantha.

"So do you think we can go on tour now?" I ask a little too loudly because I've been wearing headphones for the whole day.

She laughs because we both know it's impossible to move the tour dates up, but four months is so far away. I want to go on tour again so I don't have to think so much about Mary. I've opened up a little bit to Luca about the situation, but I don't want to talk to anyone about it. If I don't talk about it, if I ignore it long enough by going back on tour, then maybe the situation will just go away and solve themselves.

"I really think the album is amazing. Have you guys come up with a name yet?" Samantha asks.

Luca and I both look at Tony, who has named all of our albums thus far. He puts a finger to his chin, pretending to be in deep thought, but knowing him, he's been thinking about this for months now.

"*Livin'*."

"Simple," Luca starts.

"But so, so effective," I finish.

"Perfect, we'll set up a photo shoot right away." Samantha is already on her phone, scrolling frantically for the right number. She dials up the photographer and puts her pink phone to her ear, so the boys and I take this as a sign that we can take ten.

As soon as we step foot outside, I fill my lungs with as much fresh air as possible. I forget how stuffy the studio can be, especially with how tall the boys are and how much space they take up.

"See, you were stressing over nothing, Gia," Tony says. "We got the whole album done, we just have some minor tweaking to do."

I shrug my shoulders and nod. "That's the fastest I've ever written so many songs. We should celebrate tonight."

"Yep, I heard there's a new club in town that just opened, we should check it out," Luca says.

I take a dramatic step back and put my hand to my chest. "I love the way you think," I beam.

Luca rolls his eyes, draping his arm around me. I smile up at him, fully aware that I'm going to develop neck problems if I keep looking up at him. His face is just so *addicting*.

"Oh," Tony says, pulling out his phone that just buzzed. "Samantha says to go back inside." I hold down a scoff, shouldn't I be the one to decide when I go back? I bite my tongue and trudge back into the studio with the boys; we've made great progress today, I'm not about to ruin the giddy feeling buzzing in the atmosphere.

Those days when I'm literally banging my head against the wall because no ideas are coming to me and the boys' suggestions, although they are trying to help, make me dread my life. So I get really happy when things come together with a snap of my fingers and my writer's block is gone.

"Sit down, we have some new things to discuss," Samantha announces, finishing the last sip of her coffee.

Between her word choice and the alcohol in my bloodstream, my heart kicks into overdrive as I think of the worst possible scenario. My throat bobbles as I try and swallow away my worries, but the change in mood hits me like a truck driving full speed.

She clears her throat before going on. "We are going to start doing things differently. You guys have always been unique, since being in the industry at such a young age has had their pros and cons, but now that you guys are nearly twenty-two, we have to start changing."

Luca catches my eyes and shoots me a reassuring smile. How is he always so calm? I guess we balance each other out. Me, all nerves and adrenaline and impulsiveness. Him, all calm, cool and collected.

"I'll get to the point," she says. *That would be nice.* "Starting tomorrow, you guys will be with a personal trainer for six out of the seven days of the week. You guys will have to have great endurance for how many shows you have coming up, and considering how extreme you want to take your performances, we've hired a personal trainer to travel with you guys."

I zone out, my heart racing, my chest heaving. It won't be my old trainer- the one who saved my life- it's going to be some random trainer who doesn't even know me. Well, he or she will know *about* me, but they won't know me like how my old one did.

"It's going to be about an hour a day, preferably in the morning."

"Gia doesn't even roll out of bed until 11 AM," Luca laughs lightly.

I don't even argue because I know he's right.

"Well, when you guys stay out until 4 AM," Samantha digs, "it's no surprise that you guys don't wake up late."

"Technically, the bars close at 2," Tony corrects. He's such a little shit, I love him.

She continues going on about our new schedule and it goes as follows:

We wake up at 6 AM, have breakfast and whatever protein shake we want. Then, we go to the gym to train with Wendy, the new trainer, for an hour. We will then shower, head to the studio and record for a while, and then we will have a quick break for lunch.

Then we will go out- in a presentable manner, she emphasizes- and make sure to gain some more press attention. She says this is important for growing our fan base, and the thought of that makes me excited, despite the fact that we will willingly have to frame photos of us. She says she needs more "Luca- and Gia-content" because for a while we were one the of the cutest couples in Hollywood, but lately fans haven't seen us as close together.

It's not like I don't love Luca, because I obviously do, but we're past the honeymoon stage. I don't need to hold his hand 24/7, even though I don't protest when he reaches for me. I don't need to be draped over him like I used to be; we're comfortable with each other that we don't need to do all that PDA stuff.

She says she wants our face on everything- commercials, charity work, billboards, the whole nine yards.

"You guys are history in the making, I hope you know that," she says once she's gone through the never ending list.

"I'm so excited," I say, and I mean it. This is going to be a huge point in my career. For the most part, I've felt like the industry still sees us as immature kids, and sure, Tony might be the reason they think that, but it's time people take us seriously.

"Are you guys excited to start meeting more people that you listened to growing up?" she asks, seeming more excited than us.

I shoot my eyes down and don't respond. After how disappointed I was with John Feton, I'm worried that everyone else is going to disappoint me.

Chills run down my spine as I think back to John not even bothering to hide his wandering eyes on live television. "Yeah," I offer weakly.

She stands up, indicating that work is done for the day, which means we get to go out soon. "I won't lie, the next couple of months are going to be jammed-packed. Welcome to Hollywood, guys."

I shiver, the last time she said those words was when the whole John situation happened. I'm nervous, I'm excited, but ultimately, I'm scared to mess up now that I will be considered a real celebrity.

I'm not a kid anymore, I haven't been for a while, but the world has started to clue into that now, putting more pressure on us to not misstep on this tightrope.

Chapter 28

SAMANTHA WAS RIGHT, the last four months have been a total shit show. I'm tired. I'm drained and slowly losing motivation. It's been four months of not talking to Mary, it's been four months of drinking, working, and partying to forget her.

I just want to get this tour started with. The work we put into this album has almost killed me. I'm so excited to tour, especially since we are going to be in Europe.

Since the release day, *Livin'* has been the number one album for weeks. I'm so happy I want to cry, but I know that those chart numbers didn't come with us just having some luck, it came from hard work.

To make everything better, it's been nominated for a Grammy, and we will find out tomorrow if we won or not. So all the long hours have been worth it.

I honestly think I'm crashing down on my face right now because I've been working nonstop for months, and now that I'm finally sitting down for the first time in months, everything is catching up to me. I need to remember I'm not a teenager anymore; I can't do the things I used to do.

But I'll get enough sleep when I'm dead. There's only so many more years for it to be acceptable for me to be partying every night. I told the boys that when we're on stage we should act like how we do in the clubs: wild.

I'm dancing on tables, pressing my body so tight to Luca's, dancing like nobody's watching, I'm just living life; hence the album *Livin'*.

The thing that gets me, though, is that we recorded most of *Livin'* in one day, and while I understand why we had to go back and edit things, I don't understand why we've already started working on the next album.

Reen keeps pushing our due dates up, and I keep trying to push them back. Luckily, the next album isn't supposed to come out for another year, it's due to release on June 13; I'm really excited, but I don't have any set plans for it yet.

I've thrown out a couple ideas about what the main concept should be, but nothing is really coming together.

Luca nudges me on the shoulder slightly, and I'm pretty sure the microphone picks up the sound. I shake my head and blink rapidly. "Sorry, could you repeat that?"

We're sitting behind a giant wall with *Livin'* written all over it doing an interview, and I'm having a hard time hearing all of the questions.

The brunette lady stands up again and smiles. "No worries, I was just asking what is so special about this album?"

The words rush out of me before I have a chance to think if what I'm saying sounds proper. "I think fans can really see the development of Insieme in a musical sense. You can see how our perspectives on life have changed, how much we've grown, how far we've come, and the fans have grown with us too."

She sits back down with a gigantic smile on her face. I force out a smile, though I'm burning under the harsh lights that are shining.

"Next question," someone who I assume works for Reen says.

This time, a male stands up. "I want to talk about the album cover."

"Sorry, I'm going to stop you right there," Tony interrupts. "Where did you get your shirt? I love it so much." I squint my eyes to get a better look at the man, who is wearing a button up light gray shirt. I think there are bananas on it, but they might be pineapples... maybe yellow dogs? I can't tell.

"Oh." The man blushes and looks down at his shirt. "I think it's from the Old Navy."

Tony nods his head approvingly and leans into his microphone. "I love shopping there. Sorry, please continue."

The interviewer laughs and then clears his throat. "I just want to talk about the album cover choice," he continues. "For the most part, you guys have chosen to go with a neutral face, but this is the first album cover where you guys are smiling, why is that?"

Tony, eager as always, takes this one. "Well, we wanted to show the world that we really are just normal people just living. Sometimes people can get caught up in the fact that we are 'celebrities' and they think we are some sorta superhuman, but that really isn't the case. We wanted to show that we are genuine people- with genuine feelings- and we are truly just living our lives."

I smile on the inside at his answer; he could not have said that any better.

The guy who asked the question looks satisfied enough with the answer, but his eyes linger on Tony a moment longer than necessary. I catch a glance at Tony, who is still smiling at the man.

"I'm sorry, I know you get asked this a lot." It's another girl's turn to ask a question.

Luca leans into his microphone with a smirk on his face. "Then don't ask it."

The audience gives the laughter Luca was looking for, causing Luca to sit back in his chair with a proud smile on his face.

She blushes and says, "You and Giovanna have been together for so long, how do you do it? We don't see any fights, any of that, but yet you guys are still going strong."

Luca leans forward again with a smug look on his face, almost as if he was expecting this question. I know I expected it, considering we are asked that everyday.

"I would be lying if I told you it has all been rainbows and sunshine," he starts, and I feel my whole body tense up. We all know that I crave the spotlight, but I really don't like talking about Luca and I's personal life, "but she has matched every step with me in this journey. Yes, we started our puppy love when we were 16, but I wouldn't want to do this with anyone else. Giovanna is my best friend, not just my girlfriend."

I smile and nod, just like I've been trained to do, but then the girl turns to me as if she's waiting for me to respond, daring me to speak. "Right, and I think it's just important to say that we are just like normal couples- we fight, we bud heads, we clash, but we still love each other at the end of the day."

In fact, we're fighting right now. Well, not really fighting, more like... disagreeing? Here is the thing, I am the extrovert in this relationship. I want to be out, I want to drink, I want to party, I want to do all that stuff before I get too damn old for all of it. I don't want to waste all my good years. Luca wants to work on this new album day and night, all day every day. Lately, his new thing is to drop his head and give me a pouting face and say my name in a condescending tone whenever I suggest we go out.

Naturally, I end up winning every night. But sometimes, he gets so stuck in his ways, and I get so stuck in mine, that I end up going out without him. Sometimes I go with Tony, but even he sides with Luca sometimes so I end up just going to a bar by myself and having a conversation with a random bartender.

I live in Hollywood, for crying out loud. I'm
not spending every night locked up in my room
trying to write an album and crying myself to sleep
because I miss my best friend. Shouldn't we let this
album run its course before releasing the next one
anyway?

We answer about three more questions
before we thank everyone and get up to leave. I
grab my big sunglasses, which have now been
replicated in so many stores so people can look like
me. I smile at the thought that so many girls and
boys want to be like me.

I blow a huge bubble with my gum, letting it
pop loudly. This only makes Luca sigh, clearly
annoyed.

I look at him up and down with half a frown
on my face. "Am I bothering you?" It was just a
bubble.

"No, I'm used to you being loud."

I roll my eyes, thankful my glasses cover my
blush. "Let's just go home."

The car ride is spent in silence. It's not that Insieme is fighting, we've been around each other so much, it's just that we are so tired of everything.

"Where are you going tonight, Gia?" Luca asks in a neutral tone literally two blocks away from our house.

Tony sits up a bit taller, copying my actions. "Wherever you would like."

"*Amore*," he whispers. "Let's just stay in tonight."

I throw my head back against the car seat. "One day, we will be too old for all of this. And why did you even ask if you wanted to stay in?"

"But you need to slow down. You've been going harder and harder every night, coming home later and later. It's money going down the drain."

I ball my hand into a fist at my side before reaching for my bottle. At this point, I'm sure the boys know I fill this water bottle with whatever alcohol I feel like in the morning. It gets me through the day. Some people drink energy drinks, some people have coffee every morning, so how is this any different? I'm not committing a crime.

"You are more than welcome to come with me," I say. I cross my arms and purse my lips, indicating that I'm mad at him.

"Maybe." So that means *no*.

We finally get home, and Tony is trying to ease the tension by some small talk. "I thought that guy was really cute, the one who asked about our album cover."

I throw myself down on the couch and drop my jaw. "I knew that was what you were thinking! You never look at anyone that long."

"I should have gotten his number," Tony says. "I guess I should hop in the shower."

So I take that as a sign he is coming out with me tonight. He practically runs out of the room, and I'm kind of jealous of him. The tension between Luca and I is running so high and tight right now that you could cut it with a knife, and not the romantic kind of tension.

No, this is the I'm-so-mad-at-you-because-you-never-consider-me type of tension.

Luca clears his throat, making his way over to me, forcing me to make room for him. "I'm starting to feel like your babysitter."

I look him dead on. "I never asked you to be."

He looks away, clearly hurt by my bluntness. I know we're both annoyed with each other right now, but I still love him and I don't want to see him hurt. "I'm responsible for my own actions and you're responsible for your own; we can't control each other."

He looks back at me. "I meant what I said in the interview today, the thing about you always being there for me. Lately, I just feel as though you don't really have any time for me now."

"We're all busy, Luca. What do you want from me?"

"You're not busy enough to go out every night! You're not making time for, but you're making time for everything else. Aren't you the one who got mad at me last tour when I wasn't giving you enough attention?"

I shake my head. "Luca."

"Giovanna."

"I'm just asking you to love me, please. Do you know how hard it is to be in a relationship with someone who isn't that interested in the first place? You were going out with someone else, so I hope you can understand that I need a little bit of validation from you."

I can feel my heart break right in the middle. I could give him this big apology about how I've just gotten so wrapped up with my work, but that wouldn't do much. I need him. "I'm sorry."

I wrap my legs around him, planting a passionate kiss on his lips. I run my fingers through his soft, curly hair, as I breathe in his familiar scent. His mouth is desperate against mine.

"I love you, *amore*."

I pull back from his lips a bit so I can look him in the eyes. "I love you, too. I always have and I always will."

He pulls me closer by my waist, keeping a hand on my hip. "I need you in my life, Gia. I *need* you."

"I'm not going anywhere," I assure him. "I'm right here."

Things have been so up and down with us lately because we're both under a tremendous amount of stress, but I'll always go back to him. I'll always need him.

"I'm sorry I've been so hard on you lately," he says, his hands moving up and down my back. "I don't want you getting into any trouble, that's all. I'm protective of you because I want the best for you."

I put my finger to his lips. "Stop," I breathe. "It's okay."

He shakes his head, tears threatening at the corners of his eyes. "I hate fighting with you."

I let out a laugh before I lean in and kiss him again. "We're all tired, we're all drained, it's okay."

He runs his fingers through my curls, which have grown a significant amount recently; it's around my lower-back. "You're right, though. I've been so caught up in my work that I'm forgetting to have fun."

I give him a devilish smile. "That's why we're out here, Luca. Yeah, the music and all that is great, but we can't forget to have fun."

He chuckles softly. His voice has gotten significantly deeper as well, and I didn't even think it was possible, but he has grown a little bit more too. "Besides, we need something to sing about."

I cup his face in both my hands and gawk my eyes. "Now you're talking!"

"We also need to have a couple great stories to tell when we're older."

I file that thought in the back of my mind, that could be a catchy song. "I don't even want to think about getting old."

He kisses me softly this time. "It feels like yesterday we were drunk in Tony's basement having the most awkward kiss known to man-kind."

I cringe at the memory. "How did we even end up tangled with each other?"

"Seriously? You don't remember? I thought you were pretending to forget because you were embarrassed."

I shrug my shoulders. "Well… I mean, it was so long ago."

He smiles at the memory, his eyes looking through me. He's right back in that moment. "You were drunk, and at the time, you would be the chatty-drunk. A few hours before Tony fell asleep, you got mad at us and stormed into the washroom."

I suddenly feel the need to get defensive. "You just assumed I was okay with putting myself out there." The fact that the views on our first video still goes up everyday blows my mind.

Luca guides me so we can lay down, my ear directly on top of his rapid heart. "Yes, and so it was this whole episode. Anyways, when Tony fell asleep, you decided to open up to me about how much you hated your body." I tense at the reminder of my lack of confidence. It isn't there anymore, but every now and then it will slip through the cracks of the wall I have built up over the years.

Here's one thing you learn quickly when you go into Hollywood at 16: you *must* have thick skin or you will get crushed.

"I hated hearing you talk like that. You called yourself fat, and that made my heart hurt. It made me mad, actually. I was so upset that you couldn't see just how gorgeous you are. I had to sit there and listen to you talk about how you were bullied in middle school- all the awful things people would call you and how those words never left your mind.

"I didn't want you to feel like that anymore. I realized that I had to get over my nerves and I just sort of leaned in. What made me upset is that I've always found you beautiful. I know we didn't go to the same school, but we saw each other at those big banquets, and I never had the guts to tell you how much I liked you."

I look up at him. How did I get so lucky? While it's true I've learned to love myself, I would be lying if I said Luca didn't help with that. I started to feel beautiful after we started dating because he was always reminding me. He looks at me as if he's just won the lottery.

"I know that you deal with so much, and if I could go back in time and punch every single person who bullied you, I would. But that's not really possible, so I try to show my love for you in different ways."

I don't even bother to wipe tears away; I just kiss him. A long, passionate kiss; the kind you see in romance movies. The one where they are kissing in the rain after not seeing each other for five years. That's what this feels like. It's as though Luca and I have been separated our whole lives.

I pull back a bit. "I'm so sorry for how I acted the next morning. I was just a kid and I was so confused, but I am so sorry, you didn't deserve that.

Those are days we can never get back, and I don't
know if I'll ever be able to forgive myself for that."
I kick myself everyday because I know Luca and I
couldn't been together longer if I wasn't so stupid.

"You were fragile, I don't blame you for
protecting your heart. It's no surprise you were so
guarded though, you had to go through so much."

It's true. Everyday when I looked in the
mirror, I would just hear my peer's voices in my
head. They would call me things like *pig* or *ogre*
and just plain *ugly*. I don't think any girl or boy
should have to go through that. I don't *want* anyone
to feel the pain I felt.

Because I'll tell you this much: I'm sure
they said those things to fit in and hide their own
insecurities, but I believed whatever came out of
their mouth. I truly believed I was incapable of
being loved because they made me think I was so
disgusting. So unlovable. They treated me like a
disease. Always the last choice, and even then, I
was never good enough.

But look at me now.

"Luca," I whisper.

"Yes, *amore*."

"Thank you."

"For what?"

I give him a weak smile. "For saving my life."

Chapter 29

I WOKE UP TO Tony's camera shoved in my face because Luca and I fell asleep on the couch after a long night out. It's become routine at this point, and I think the fans are more excited to get another Instagram photo more than anything. Half of the comments are like "they definitely just want to make us jealous", but we just want to show ourselves without makeup on. We want to show that we are normal too, just like Tony said in the interview.

"I'm going to puke," I announce, bolting for the washroom. Nothing comes out, I just end up dry heaving the butterflies out of my stomach.

I'm so nervous for tonight. What if we don't win? I know that getting nominated for a Grammy is the end all be all, and I'm so thankful to even be in this position, but I can't get all dressed up and not win. That's just embarrassing if we leave empty handed.

"Gia, you have to eat something. You can't go to Reen on an empty stomach," Tony comments.

"I'm too nervous to eat."

So many cameras. So many people. So many of my role models. So many judging eyes. I don't even know if I want to wear the dress we have picked out. Although our music has changed and grown with us throughout the years, our color coordinating outfits have stayed.

Tony and Luca take their time eating, even though they know I want to get out the door as fast as possible. I'm looking forward to seeing Kassie the most- she's become one of my favorite people in the industry. We get each other's humor and I genuinely enjoy her company; she calms me down before going on stage.

Eventually, the boys finish eating and I'm practically dragging them out the door. Seriously, why are they so slow today? They know I want to make sure everything is perfect. Millions of people are going to be seeing me, and that means only one thing.

I need to get a drink. There is absolutely no way I'm getting into a $40,000 dress without my confidence booster. The dress the designers picked out is a bold red with a gold belt. It has a sweetheart neckline and hugs me tight at the top and flares out like a ball gown at the bottom with the gold shimmery belt to tie in the look.

I feel like a princess in it. I look like a princess in it, but still, there is nothing wrong with a confidence boost.

"Okay, we're in the car now, you need to relax," Luca says gently.

I can't stop my leg from shaking, in fact, my whole body is shaking. I'm trying to calm down, but there's just plenty of emotions running high in my blood stream right now that I don't even know how to breathe properly.

"I'm sorry," I peep.

It's only about a ten minute car ride, but it feels like an hour has passed by the time I'm bursting through the doors. To my delight, Samantha is just as tizzy as I am, which means the boys are crazy for being this calm.

"Okay. Everything needs to run *smoothly*." I don't know why she's looking at me when she says that, but I let her go on and do her little lecture. "There's one thing I want to get clear."

"Hit us," Luca says.

"Even if you don't win tonight, I'm proud of you." Is that a voice break I just heard? "I know how much work we've been putting on you recently, but look how it's paying off. I know that they were excruciating days, but you guys pushed through and now you can officially say that you are a Grammy nominated trio."

My heart swells. Sometimes I wonder if Samantha really does enjoy working with us because she can come off as annoyed, but she's just trying to get everything organized for us. It feels really, really good to hear the P word come out of her mouth.

Something I've learnt over my time here is this: I can't get enough compliments. No matter how many times someone says they think I'm amazing, I love to hear it. I encourage it. People say

"I know you hear this a lot" and I do hear it a lot, but dammit, tell me I'm great one more time. It feels *good*.

What doesn't feel good is not being able to breathe on an airplane when I'm just trying to see my family, but they are just fans and they don't know any better; they don't mean any harm.

"Getting nominated was already the victory, but let's hope to come home with that trophy tonight, okay?" Is that a tear in her eye I see?

Before I can even think twice, I'm making my way over to her and hugging her. "Thank you," I say against her straight blonde hair. "Thank you for everything you've done and continue to do for me."

Yes, I'll be the first one to tell you that the three of us were the ones who built our fanbase. We worked hard, we put ourselves out there, and while other people would've gotten cold feet, our feet were sizzling.

But Samantha is the one who picked up the phone. She recognized our talent, she knew we just had *it*, and she was betting on us in hopes that we would double down and do the work. So, yes, I think of Samantha as my Hollywood Fairy Godmother.

"Okay, okay, that's enough before I start to cry," she says.

She runs through exactly how tonight is going to go. She stresses that we smile at everyone we see, no matter if we like them or not. We are to smile until our cheekbones feel like they are going to fall right off. Smile and nod, smile and nod, smile and nod.

Seems simple enough. Except I can't stand some bitches.

"Giovanna, I am begging you, please sit nicely. You're always like, I don't know, man spreading whenever you're in the studio. Please sit with your legs together," she comments once she's gone through all the major points.

Luca scoffs. "She's always been such a classy lady."

"Oh, you're in love with her, shut up," Tony teases.

"I'm sure it won't even matter, my dress is going to be covering my legs," I reason.

Samantha shakes her head and smiles. "What do you have against sitting with your legs together?"

"It's uncomfortable!" I state. "My ankles are touching and that's just such a weird sensation going through my ankle bones. Plus, I'm so focused on keeping my legs together that they start to move apart!"

"You do it in interviews." She crosses her arms. I love when we get like this: when we fight over stupid things and both of us are too stubron to stop.

"That's cause fucking John Feton would be staring."

She cocks her eyebrows. "So you won't do it for the Grammys? People care way more about the Grammys than they do about that loser."

"Fine."

"Now that Gia is done being so complicated, you guys need to go to your designers and artists to get ready in time."

And that's when the real chaos happens. I don't see the boys for hours. So many people are pulling and slicking back my mess of curls into a tight low ponytail with just a few curly strands in the front.

"That hurts!" I yelp. "Kassie, I really wanted to wear my hair down."

She shakes her head and tsks. "With the type of neckline your dress has, this will look better. Trust me, sweetheart."

"What if you left half the hair down and pulled half of it back with a clip," I suggest, making my eyes big in the mirror as I look at her.

She stops what she's doing so everyone else stops too. "Gia, I love ya, I really do, but don't *ever* try to tell me how to do my job."

I put my tail between my legs and shoot my eyes to the ground. "It's just that my curls are my signature."

She laughs but there isn't any amusement behind it. "Think about it this way: everyone will get to see your gold hoops."

I shrug my shoulders. "Okay, sorry."

She's just stressed, I tell myself. There is no need to worry, she'll be back to normal once the Grammys are all done. I hope so. I can't lose another close friend, not now.

"I hope we win," I say, trying to start a conversation.

She looks at me in the mirror. "If you don't win, then I will go and sue the Grammys myself." And she's back.

I let out a hearty laugh. "I'm so nervous, Kassie. I've been dry heaving all day, I can't sit still, nothing is working out with my looks."

"Just breathe with me really quickly." She forces me to match her deep breathing. Inhale, two, three. Exhale, two, three.

She's satisfied with my ponytail by the time I've calmed down. "My work here is done, now the wardrobe crew are going to be here in about twenty minutes."

"And then it's red carpet time," I finish for her. I've ran through the schedule fifty times today.

"Exactly! Now give me a hug." I stand up and embrace her, inhaling her sweet perfume that is much too strong for this tight space. It's a huge room, actually, but there's just too many people.

"Thanks, Kassie," I call as she closes the door.

"You're welcome!" Kassie yells back from the other side.

I wait five seconds. I dash to my back pack that I always bring with me and pull out my flask. I take off the lid and tilt my head all the way back as I down the whiskey.

So sweet, so smooth, so much *confidence*.

I can already feel my heartbeat kick into overdrive and a happy buzz wash over me. I march over to the mirror and place both hands down on the vanity and start talking to myself.

"Giovanna Rossi, you are the most gorgeous girl I have ever seen," I say to myself. "Look at how far you've come; you're Grammy nominated! You know what? I think you'll win. Insieme is top of the charts right now, of course you deserve this. Bring it home."

A knock on the door sends me spinning around, nearly knocking over the chair in the process. "Come in."

The chaos comes rushing in. I step into the huge dress, it's very over the top, but it's the Grammys, afterall.

"Is there any way I can keep that on?" I ask as one of the workers reaches for Lorenzo's bracelet.

"We have this one for you, ma'am," she responds, holding up a bulky gold bracelet. It's beautiful and designer, but it's not me. It's not my lucky bracelet.

I give her a small smile, trying to sound as nice as possible. "I would just prefer to wear this one." She looks at me as if I have three heads on my shoulders. "It's my lucky bracelet," I explain, but even as I say it, it sounds ridiculous that I would refuse such a gorgeous bracelet. "I haven't taken it off since the day I got it."

She looks like she's holding in a laugh. "But, ma'am, this is Versace."

I want to scream because I really just want to hurry this process up, but I remain calm. I try to, at least. "That doesn't matter, I would prefer to wear this bracelet."

She opens and closes her mouth several times before she finally says, "I don't think your bracelet goes with the outfit."

I look at myself in the mirror. This beautiful dress hugs me in all the right places, and Kassie was right, my hair style ties everything together. I look down at the small bracelet I was gifted with when I was 16 and then look back at the lady. "I think it goes well with the gold belt."

"But I think this one will look better."

I flare out my nostrils and purse my lips together. I don't raise my voice, I drop it to a whisper. "Well, you're not the one going on the red carpet, are you?"

She drops her head. "I'm just doing my job."

"No, you're not, actually. *Your* job is to make *me* happy- and let me tell you- you're not doing a good job."

She swallows hard. "What's so special about that stupid bracelet anyways that you can't take it off for the Grammys?"

I gawk my eyes at her. "I think it's time you leave. I don't have to explain anything to you and I can put on my own jewelry. You're of no use here."

She opens her mouth to say something again, and I'm about to punch her teeth out to save her the embarrassment, but Tony and Luca come rushing it. "You're still getting ready?" Tony asks. "Even I'm ready, I take forever."

I flash them a smile. "I'm actually ready." I turn myself towards the workers, but look at the lady head on. "That will be all, thank you. Oh, and before you go, what was your name?"

"Hailey."

"Hailey, I don't want you on this crew anymore."

"But-"

"Go."

And she does, they all do. I take a shaky breath, it's not that I feel bad, but I've never really gotten mad like that. I pride myself in being nice to everyone so people can see I'm just like them, and to be honest, I'm worried about Miss Hailey over there running her mouth to the press and telling everyone I'm horrible to deal with.

"What was that all about?" Luca asks, grazing my arm.

I shake my head. "She wanted me to take off Lorenzo's bracelet. I couldn't, Luca, I just couldn't."

"Hey, it's okay," he whispers, pulling me closer to him but also making sure to not ruin my makeup. "I think you look beautiful, *amore*."

"Did I tell you how much I love it when you call me that," I say into his chest.

"You have, *amore*."

"Barf," Tony comments. "Okay, let's take pictures."

Tony has a red suit with a black shirt and a gold handkerchief, and Luca just switched with a black suit and red shirt. We look fierce.

Tony takes about twenty selfies and is only satisfied with one, but then he decides that he doesn't even like that one so we just decide it's time to head out and wait for pictures to be sent to us.

"Whatever happens, happens," I say, the boys have left the speech up to me, naturally. "But here's the thing, I know we're going to win. Let's just go out there and show the world that we are so hot right now."

"Damn right," Tony agrees.

"Hey, I know we've been super busy and I haven't told you guys this in a long time," Luca starts, "but I love you guys. I'm so glad I get to spend every day with my best friends, and I think we all deserve to go to the afterparty."

I smile at the thought of the afterparty, it's going to be amazing. "Yeah, you guys are pretty great," I laugh.

"Okay, but seriously, it's been my dream to walk a red carpet so can we just get out there already?" Tony asks, setting an exciting mood over us.

"Let's live out our dreams," Luca agrees

"We have been for the past four years," I whisper with a proud smile only loud enough for myself to hear.

Chapter 30

THE CAMERA LIGHTS ARE blinding and I have a serious itch on the back of my thigh, but I suppress it with a bright smile. It feels like we've been on the red carpet for hours, but I'm sure it's only been half an hour.

The three of us have been moving in perfect synchronization, posing exactly like how we were taught. I'm in the middle, of course, because if I wasn't, no one would be able to see me with my whole five feet.

"No freakin' way," Tony says once we've run our course with the cameras and the red carpet. "Is that who I think it is? Elliot Lloyd is my role model, I have to go talk to him." Before we can stop him and remind him Samantha told us to stay together, he's dashing off to Elliot.

"Luca!" I fight the urge to roll my eyes at the sound of her voice. If there's a problematic woman in Hollywood, it's Jen Pommer. It's not that she's a *bad* person, it's just that she's always telling the press how much she loves our work. And Luca. She "loves" Luca.

"Hey, Jen." Luca turns around, looping his arm smoothly in mine.

"I heard you have been nominated for Album of the Year! That's the same category as me, that's amazing! Congrats, Luca." Her strawberry blonde hair is so straight, it's gorgeous. Everyone knows she's beautiful, with her green eyes and great hair, but she is always running into trouble. She doesn't sugar coat anything and speaks her mind, but when she starts telling The Times about how much she would love to date Luca, it's hard for me to like her. She's been doing it more frequently in the last three months, so thank goodness I've been busy or else I could guarantee I would have said something to the press and there would have been a big scandal.

Luca tightens his grip on me. "The three of us worked really hard on it. Gia wrote most of the songs." Why am I blushing? It's true. I'm so awkward I want to cry.

She looks me up and down with the fakest smile I've ever seen. Gosh, if I knew I would have to deal with Miss Pommer, I would have packed two flasks.

"Is that so?" she asks.

"No, he just made it up." I curse myself as soon as the sarcastic comment leaves my mouth. So far, Tony has left us, I'm not being friendly, so I just know Samantha is going to have a lot to say after this night.

"What?"

"She was just joking," Luca says quickly, shooting me a sideways glare.

Jen laughs, putting her hand on Luca's shoulder. "You're so funny, has anyone ever told you that? Hey, are you going to the after party?"

I can't. First of all, her hand is on *my* boyfriend. Second of all, why is she laughing like that? Third of all, I can't control my breathing, she's making me so mad.

"Excuse me," I mumble, untangling myself from Luca.

I turn to my right and just start marching, even though I don't know where I am going. I pass so many celebrities, it's intimidating. It's clear that we are still so young because most people here are well over thirty. I feel awkward and out of place.

I feel like an outcast.

Breathing is getting harder and harder, sharper and sharper.

Too. Many. People.

My eyes are going crazy, back and forth, back and forth. Why can I hear my heartbeat in my ears?

I need a drink.

I need a drink.

I need a drink.

"Gia?"

"I'm fine." I just need some space.

"Gia, what's wrong?"

"Luca, I'm fine."

I need to get out of here.

So many things are going on. Too many people are talking over the loud snaps of cameras, too many interviewers are trying to get my attention, too many people want Luca, too many people are judging me.

"Can I get you something to drink?" he offers, careful to keep his distance.

I stop in my tracks. "I'd love that." I didn't know there was a bar here, but Luca is leading me there and the next thing I know, I have a glass of champagne in my hand.

Champagne never tasted so good. "Luca, thank you, I just really needed to get out of Jen's presence."

"Please, I get it. She's so aggravating." He flips imaginary hair and starts imitating Jen. *"You're so funny! Has anyone ever told you?"*

I double over as I laugh, grabbing onto Luca so I don't fall in these four inch heels. I call the bartender and order another glass of champagne. "I can't stand her."

"Who?"

I jump at the sight of an interviewer with *Entertainment Tonight!* standing right behind me, shoving a microphone in my face. "Uh…" I take another sip from my glass.

"Who can't you stand?" he presses. Who the hell is this guy and who told him that a white tuxedo looks good?

"I don't know what you're talking about." I turn around and take a bigger sip, hoping he'll get the message that I don't want to talk to him.

Of course, the paparazzi never get the hint. They're like mosquito bites, tiny and annoying and so, so irritating.

"I heard you just now," he says.

"I was talking to my boyfriend."

"But I'm sure, and I speak for everyone watching at home, that we want to know who you can't stand."

Samantha is going to kill me.

Luca steps in front of me slightly, shielding me from this guy and the camera that is following him around like a lost puppy. "That's just between us." He winks and smiles at the camera; I'm sure about two hundred teenage girls just fainted on their couch just now.

"Alright, then. Would you mind telling us how you're feeling tonight?"

Why won't he just leave us alone?

My guardian angel must be watching over me because we're all called to our seats ten seconds after he asks us.

"Looks like we better get going," Luca says, already pulling me towards our seats. I'm trailing behind Luca, hoping he knows where he's going. "Samantha told me our seats," he explains, looking over his shoulder. I nod my head and let him lead me. Tony must have gotten the memo too because he's already seated.

"How was Elliot?" I ask.

The lights dim and Tony leans into me. "I'll tell you all about it later," he whispers.

The host appears on the stage, indicating that the show is about to begin. He makes the audience laugh and I laugh with them, even if I don't really understand his jokes.

We sit through the ceremony, patiently waiting for the Album of the Year award to happen. With all the performances and all the speeches, we've been here for three and a half hours and our category has still yet to be presented. I'm overheating in this dress and I don't know how much longer I can last.

Finally, it's time for our category and the nominees video is rolling. "And the Grammy for Album of the Year goes to…"

I grasp Luca and Tony's hand so hard, I'm sure that their knuckles are white. My breathing hitches, I'm scared to breathe.

Can this lady just open the damn envelope already?

"The award goes to…"

Insieme. It *has* to be Insieme. Who else in the industry has done what we've done? There is no way it's not us.

I tighten my grip and sit on the edge of my seat. I already have a speech prepared; I can taste victory on my tongue already.

My heart beats… beats… beats. My vision is b l u r y. It has to be us.

"Livin' by Insieme!"

I jump up, pumping my fist in the air and almost knocking the boys over in the process.

"I knew it!" I yell over the applause, hugging each of the boys. Tony accepts the trophy and they clear the way for me to the microphone.

Despite the heels, they have to lower the microphone. "Thank you! I'll try and keep this short and sweet, but there are just so many people I need to thank. First off, I would like to say hi to our families watching at home. Everything you've seen us do in the past few years is because our families have loved us and supported us through every step.

"To our manager, Samantha, and to Reen, and our producer, Mike, thank you for putting up with us. I know we can be a handful sometimes, and I just want to say thank you for seeing all of our ideas through.

"To the fans." My voice breaks and I have to take a step back for a moment, Luca's hand finds my lower waist and comforts me. "You guys have been amazing. Some of you have been here since our YouTube days, and Insieme has all started because of you. We love you, we see you, and we appreciate you.

"The boys promised me I could do the speech," I laugh, "but is there anything you guys would like to add?" I turn around and raise my eyebrow at them, inviting them to speak.

Luca nods his head and steps forward. "I just want to say one thing. If you don't know this, Insieme all started because our sweet little Giovanna had a dream about it. That dream has become our reality through hard work and long days, but it has also come thanks to you guys. We would not be here without you."

Tony puts his hand on Luca's shoulder. "The fans are the backbone of this trio, and we thank you for that. We are looking forward to meeting you on our next tour!"

The applause is so loud that the sound is vibrating off the walls. I've never felt a buzz so high.

"Don't cry, you'll ruin your makeup," Luca says softly once we are back in our seats.

I let out a laugh. "We did it."

He takes my hand in his. "I always knew we would."

Tony leans over me. "How good does it feel to say that we won a Grammy?"

I let out a sigh of relief. "I'm so glad this baby is coming home with us."

"But first," Tony says, "we have an afterparty to attend to."

Chapter 31

"I DON'T REMEMBER ANYTHING after our speech." My voice is gone; it sounds like I've smoked twelve packs of cigarettes.

Luca rubs his eyes. "My head is pounding."

"Now *that* was one hell of a party," Tony says, getting up, clearly not affected at all.

"How the hell do you never get hungover?"

Tony shrugs at Luca. "You're just a lightweight."

"I'm a lightweight? Gia has one drink and she's spilling her whole guts out to the party."

"What? No I didn't!" I hope...

"You laughed right in Jen's face and told her she didn't have a chance with Luca," Tony reminds me.

"Did I?"

"Yep."

I shrug. "She had it coming."

"Uh-oh," Luca whispers, looking at his phone.

"What?"

He jumps up off the floor, grabbing anything that is in his reach. "We're going to miss our flight!"

I laugh at the sight of him. "Remember what happened the last time we didn't listen to Tony and flew on a regular plane?"

"I'm so glad you are listening to me on this one," Tony says. "The private jet is the way to go."

"It's not like we can't afford it," I add.

Luca shakes his head. "Right. Sorry, I forgot. Besides, Gia, with your anxiety about flying, I'm sure screaming fans and cameras shoved in your face don't help your situation."

Tony rolls his eyes. "Please, this girl just wants to get drunk on a plane without everyone seeing, don't let her fool you."

I shoot him a look. "Hair of the dog in about three hours?"

"Well, I can't let you drink alone," he laughs.

"We won a Grammy, we deserve it."

That's the line we say as soon as we step onto the plane, when we get another bottle of champagne, and when Luca asks if we really need all of this.

We deserve it.

I pull out my phone and text the only person who's been on my mind all day and all night.

Me: Hey Mary, long time no see! How are things?

My heart races as I see the three tiny little bubbles pop up on my screen right away as she types. They appear and disappear five times before I get:

Mary: Hey! I've been good, but I see you've been great! Congrats on your Grammy, you deserved it. I would have been pissed if that girl Jen won.

I laugh out loud at my screen, tears threatening in my tear ducts. Maybe I created this whole tension in my head, maybe everything was fine and there wasn't an issue. If I picked up the phone four months ago, would I have gotten this response? I don't know. I could have picked up the phone, but so could she. I take a deep breath and like her message and tell her I'm about to fly and I'll call her soon.

We're heading on our Europe tour, and we convinced Samantha to convince her bosses to let us stay in Italy for about three weeks. We aren't landing in Italy, though. We are going to France right now and performing for our Paris show tonight. I honestly can't even keep track of the days with my jetlag.

We're going to be ending in Italy because we are there so long. We're going to hit some of the countries in Europe: Portugal, Spain, Germany, Greece, and then finally Italy.

We're performing a maximum of two shows per country, but in Italy, we are going to do at least three shows in Rome alone. We are then going to travel to the Northern and Southern regions of our grandparents' home country. I'm ecstatic.

"Here's the thing," I say once we are checked into the hotel and I'm already a little tipsy. "This is our tour for *Livin'*."

"That's a really great point, I didn't realize that." Tony rolls his eyes with a smirk.

I'm honestly used to his comments by now, so I choose to ignore him. "So I think we should live up to the actions we sing about."

"What do you mean, *amore*?" Luca asks, leaning into me on the bed.

I cock my head to the side. "Bright lights. Crowd diving. All that stuff we were too scared to do on our first couple of albums."

Luca nods his head. "Well, we did a lot of that in our last show, but I know what you mean and I agree with you. I think it's time we let loose and have fun."

I smile and press my forehead against his, scrunching my nose. "I'm glad we're on the same page."

"This is the top floor sweet and you two *still* can't find a room," Tony says, distaste dripping out of his words.

I lean in to kiss Luca. Isn't this great? Hotel sweet, perfect boyfriend, on tour with my best friends, and we just won a Grammy. Do I dare say that my life couldn't get any better?

"Wait guys, look at this." Tony throws his phone over to us.

"I don't even want to read about us right now," Luca says, turning the phone away.

"No, this is actually funny," Tony pushes. I get up and walk over to the mini bar.

"I don't give a damn about what they have to say about me. There's always somebody who has to judge us. You can't make anyone happy, so what's the point in trying to be something you're not?" I say.

"Have you seen this post?" he asks, in awe that I knew exactly what it was about before I even glanced at it.

"No. I just know that people always have *something* to say because they really have nothing better to do. It's like those people who leave a one star Google review on a convenience store because they didn't have that much selection."

Tony drops his jaw. "I like this Giovanna."

It's the alcohol that's making me talk, but maybe this needs to come out. I've kept it all bottled up for the most part. I'm a tea kettle that's been boiling for so long and I'm about to whistle. "I just can't believe the nerve of some people. Like, do you know how much hate we got when we were literally 16-years-old? No one deserves that. But they're just looking for the next hot topic, and it's always painting us in a bad way that makes their shit sell."

"Preach."

I throw my head back and groan, downing another gulp. "Don't even get me started on 'fans' sexualizing us, especially Luca. Like there are the fans who think you're cute, and then there are the ones who just cross the line."

"I hate those edits," Luca mutters.

I swing my arms in the air. "I know! I do too! Do you think I want to see my boyfriend in a 'hot' edit?"

"I always feel like they're judging me," Luca says, ducking his head into his shoulder. He's so cute when he's shy.

I turn around way too fast, causing the room to spin. I stumble my way over to Luca, straddling him so I can maintain my balance.

"Honestly, who cares? We're twenty-three and Insieme is on top of the world. Why should we care what some journalist has to say?" I used to read all the articles on my favorite celebrities when I was younger, so it does sound a bit weird for me to say all of this, but that was before I realized that not everything you read on the internet is true.

"That's right," Tony agrees.

"We're allowed to party. What do they expect? For us to just lock ourselves in the hotel room like a bunch of seniors? No, we're going to live each day to the fullest."

I have this bubbling feeling in my stomach because I just know that this tour is going to be one to remember. I know that I will look back on these days and know that I lived life with no regrets.

Life is a party. That's how it has to be when you're on tour.

Chapter 32

"YOU TOLD US YOU were going to call everyday," Antonio says, disappointment crawling through the phone.

I rub my temples. "I know, and I'm sorry, but life got really busy."

"I get it, but, Gia, we haven't heard from you in four months."

"That's not true!" I can go back in our text history right now and show proof that I've reached out. Sure, they might have been short texts, but there was something.

"It is! I can't believe you forgot about your family," he yells.

"Don't yell at me!" I yell back. "The time change is so different here, too."

"No, I will yell at you," he fires back. "You won a Grammy, congrats, but what about us? The people who 'supported you every step of the way'? How *dare* you go up on stage and act like you talk to us everyday just to look good in the press."

"What do you want me to do?! I'm out here busting my ass, sometimes I don't have time to call you guys everyday!" Is that such a crime?

"You promised. I don't like who you're becoming."

"Of course you don't," I mumble. "Of course you can't stand to see me live *such* a bad life."

"You're drunk right now, aren't you." He doesn't ask it, he already knows. I remain silent, wanting to scream and cry. I know he's not wrong, I don't know what to say to him, so I don't say anything at all. "Gia, we're proud of you, but call us once in a while. We would like to hear your voice somewhere other than the grocery store. I still love you, we still love you, but you need to clean up your act." He hangs up before I have a chance to respond. I look at myself in the mirror, everything has changed.

For the first time I realized something before my concert tonight: I'm slowly starting to become the person I never wanted to be. But I'm too far into this to stop now.

"BELLA ROMA!" I'M LOSING my voice, but the crowd goes wild. This has got to be my favorite tour. I mean the North America tour was amazing and definitely a learning experience, but the Europe tour is just *cool*.

The fact that we've traveled across the world to hear fans scream everytime we step foot onto the stage, and their first language isn't English, it's surreal.

Insieme has tripled our network from when we started out; we're filthy rich. We have so much money, we're practically swimming in it. We each have over one million followers on all of our social media platforms, so we've been posting a lot more.

I've completely let loose on this tour. I've enjoyed being here and meeting all the fans. I don't really give a damn what the paparazzi has to say because they don't even know me. I know me, and I know that I'm living my best life, so no I don't really care what kind of articles are getting published right now. I can honestly say now that I don't check my comments anymore.

Here's the thing: all the boys want to be Luca, all the girls want to be me, and everyone wants to have Tony as their best friend.

"This song was made for a very special person," I say in between heaving breaths. (No matter how hard I train, cardio is still very hard). I don't even know if they can understand English, but the crowd roars back in response. It makes me smile, despite the depressing emotions swirling around in my gut at the moment.

"I wonder who that could be," Luca snickers into the microphone, walking to stand next to me.

If it wasn't painfully obvious I was in love with Luca to the press, I made it very clear this tour. There have been so many edits that pop up on my phone of us dancing on top of each other on stage.

I've always felt so ugly. I used to think that no one could ever love me because I was just too awkward, too different. I didn't know that I was capable of loving one person so much, and I didn't know that someone could have so much unconditional love for me.

"Here's 'More Than a Crush' for you!" I announce as soon as the music starts playing.

I don't know how to explain it, but it's like I completely transform when I'm singing on stage. As if I was born for this. I wouldn't want to be doing anything else, despite all the doubts and trials I've had to face. Insieme won a Grammy, for crying out loud. Yes, I got into a fight with my brother before going on stage, but none of that matters right now.

This is an upbeat song, and I'm jumping so much that I think I might break the stage underneath my feet. The fans in the floor seats are reaching their sweaty arms higher and higher for me to touch. The security guards are trying their best to push them back, so I can't really touch their hands. I know I have the potential to cause so many memories if I were to just touch my hand to theirs, but the security guards are depriving fans of that.

I look at Tony, who is having the time of his life. He's dancing around like a maniac, but no one is judging him, they're admiring him. Well, Luca is laughing as he's singing because he's trying to mimic Tony, but it's in a loving and endearing way.

I look at the boys. I look at the crowd. I feel the alcohol sloshing around in my stomach. I flash a smile to the crowd. The crowd screeches with laughter. Someone calls out, "You're my role model!" Another person says, "I love you!" I yell, "I love you, too!"

I turn around so my back is to the crowd, inching closer to the edge. I catch Luca's worried eyes and silently tell him that this is okay. I hear everyone hold their breath; they must know what's coming.

I mean, give the people what they want, right?

I fall back. The crowd catches me. I'm overcome with an uncontrollable burst of laughter. Life is good. So many clammy hands are carrying me around the crowd touching the bottom of my blue blouse. I'm soaring. Literally. So many phones, so many flashes, so many fans. So much adrenaline.

I should do this every show.

I crane my neck to the stage, where the boys are standing awestruck. I guess we've never really discussed doing this, they probably didn't expect it.

"*Ti amo, Roma!*"

I don't ever want to leave. I love performing, I love this album, I love Insieme. Yes, I know that the due date for the next album is creeping up on me, but I'm sure I can get an extension. I mean, Reen would be absolutely stupid to unsign us just because they can't wait a couple more weeks.

I've been so busy, and I will not let some manger sit there and tell me to work faster. Masterpieces take time. So for now, I'm just going to enjoy my time in Italy; it's my vacation.

I *deserve* it.

Chapter 33

FOR THE FIRST TIME in months, I pick up Mary's phone call on the first ring.

"I'm worried about you."

"Why?"

Mary goes silent on the other line. I would complain that this is costing too much money, since it's a long distance call and she should just hurry up and say what she needs to say, but I can afford it. Whether she can or not, I'll cover the cost anyway.

"Giovanna, what are you doing right now?" she finally asks.

I put her on speaker phone. "I'm getting ready to go to the club," I say, as if she should already know. I mean, the whole world knows I go out every night, so how can she not know?

She lets out a huff. "Exactly. I'm worried about you."

I stiffen, pausing in the middle of putting on my hoop earrings. "What is that supposed to mean?"

I can just envision her ticking off her fingers one by one as she lectures me. "You're going out every day, you're going absolutely insane on stage. Since when do you start grinding on Luca with a smile on your face, are you not embarrassed that your parents see that? And since when do you crowd dive? Giovanna, I'm worried about you."

"I'm having fun," I fire back harshly, getting defensive.

I can hear her laugh. "You're pushing the limits. This isn't the Giovanna I remember."

"Why are you getting mad at me right now? You're the one who told me to go to LA."

"Don't raise your voice at me," she warns. "I'm your best friend. I know you and this isn't healthy."

"Best friends don't ghost each other for months," I point out matter-of-factly, neither blaming her or myself.

"I know, but-"

"You don't know shit," I interrupt, practically spitting into the phone. "You can't just call me and start judging me. You don't know what it's like to have so many people watching you and putting expectations on you. I have an album to write, and after the success we saw with *Livin'* there are high expectations for the next one. Guess what? I have no idea what I'm going to write about."

"And going out every night is the right solution? What does Luca have to say about this?"

"Mary, we haven't talked in so long and all you're doing is judging me." I twirl around in the mirror, making sure everything is perfectly smooth.

"No, Gia, I call *you*, but *you* never call me back."

"You know how busy I've been," I say, getting even more defensive.

"I'm just surprised you even picked up my phone call."

"Do you think I just see your name and automatically decline the call?" I take a step back as if she can see me.

"That's how I've felt lately. How are you busy, exactly? You're a singer." I can see her scrunch her face because she used to do that all the time when she didn't understand something.

My jaw cracks as I drop it. "I don't know, let me think. Commercials, sponsors, interviews, writing albums, and, wait let me think, touring."

"Oh, you poor thing, you must have *such* a hard life."

"You know what? I was excited to talk to you, but you're being so judgemental."

She scoffs. "I'm tired of not hearing from my 'best friend' for months and then having to act like I'm okay with that. The fame is going to your head. You don't have any limits."

I pause for a moment, realizing where this is all coming from. "You read all that shit they put out about me, don't you?" She doesn't answer, she must think it's a rhetorical question. "Hello?"

Her voice is smaller now. "Yeah."

I shake my head. "Mary, please don't do that. You can't trust anything they say about me."

"They have pictures."

"Okay..?"

She lets out a disappointed sigh. "Can you honestly tell me you're not drinking yourself stupid every night?" This time it's me who doesn't answer her question. "That's what I thought."

My voice cracks. "Mary, please, it helps me."

"With what? Giovanna, you should hear how stupid you sound! You have everything you've ever wanted; you have so much and people have so little. How *spoiled*. What is there not to like? You don't have any problems, your life isn't that bad, so stop with all the drama."

"You don't understand," I start.

"Because I'm not as famous as you, yeah, remind me one more time."

A tear runs down my cheek. I can't lose Mary. I can't. "I'm on a strict schedule during the day. Reen is putting us through so much training, almost three hours a day now. I have to watch what I eat. I can't leave my house without being dressed up, but I'm a normal person, sometimes I want to go to the store in my sweatpants."

"G, I know it's different, but it can't be that bad."

I want to say *you don't understand*, but I stop myself. "We've got recording equipment on the tour bus now. They've started making us record, even though we're on tour. Do you know how hard that is on our vocal cords?"

"But you seem so happy," she says.

I give her a laugh. "I mean, I can't explain it. I love my job, I really do, but I'm just saying that I do so much throughout the day that I think I deserve to blow off some steam at night."

She sputters a bit, trying to find the right words. "I... I talked to Luca. I told him to keep an eye on you because I'm worried and I'm not there to watch you."

"Mary." I don't need to be watched, I'm a grown adult.

"Because I don't want your drinking to get out of hand. When you came over to my house to tell me you were leaving, you absolutely reeked of alcohol. Everyone knows you were intoxicated when you were performing at your uncle's restaurant, so I *know* that you're drunk during your concerts."

She's not wrong, so I don't say anything.

"I've always been your number one supporter. You're like a sister to me and I wish we were as close as we used to be, but you chose the fame. You wanted your name on billboards, and props to you for making that happen. But I don't think we should talk for a while."

"Mary, I don't want to lose you," I plead, my hands shaking as I bring them to my head. "I don't want to lose you again." So much blood is rushing to my brain that I have to take a seat on the floor or else I'll pass out.

"You don't call me. You don't check up on me. You haven't even asked me if I've gotten in a relationship or if I've figured out my career. You don't care about me. You chose to let me go. You pushed me to this point; you brought this on yourself."

"I'm sorry-"

"Goodbye, Giovanna."

The call disconnects.

I am d i z z y.

I am FUMING.

My mind is blank. How can I be soaring so high that I can almost touch the sky and then I get one phone call and now I'm
spiraling,

    spiraling

        down,

            down,

                D

                    O

                        W

                          N.

There's a knock on the bathroom door, followed by Luca's voice. "Gia, are you going out?"

I swing the door open, nearly knocking Luca over because I didn't realize he was leaning on it. "Mary called you."

"Yeah, a few days ago," he says truthfully, as if he doesn't see anything wrong with it.

I can feel my tears starting again, and at this point, I don't even care about my makeup smudging. "Are you worried about me?"

He rubs the back of his neck and his face turns beat red. "A little," he whispers.

"Look at me."

His eyes meet mine. "Tony and I will be done for the night, but you just want to keep going. You drink so much, Gia. All day. Everyday. I'm a little worried."

I give him a cold snicker. "You're more than welcome to stay home, but you choose to go out." I'm sick and tired of people acting as if I'm the only one who goes out.

"You used to get mad at me when I didn't go out," he points out. "And I want to spend time with you."

"You know what you should be concerned about?" I ask, walking back into the bathroom.

"What, *amore*?" he asks with a smug smile on his face, as if he's amused by my anger.

"You should be concerned about the fact that we've been dating for almost five years and you still haven't gotten down on one knee." I slam the bathroom door shut and start to wipe off my makeup. I take off my hoops and slip out of my dress and back into my sweatpants and hoodie. I do this all while ignoring the banging of Luca's fist on the door.

I open the door and march to grab my purse and wallet. "I'll be back," I mutter to Tony, who's sitting confused on the bed.

"Gia, wait." Luca grabs my elbow.

"I just need some space," I say without looking at him.

He squints his eyes at me. "Where are you going?"

"Out."

"Let me come with you. Let me talk to you."

"No."

"Giovanna, please."

"I'll be back," I say and he lets go of me. I walk towards the door and I turn around to look at him. "I already have enough eyes on me, I especially don't need your judgmental ones watching me." I grab my ball cap before heading out the door.

I walk and walk and walk. The tears flow and flow and flow. There's only one thing left for me to do.

I find myself a bar and I order a drink.

Chapter 34

I HAVE LOST COUNT of how much I've had, but I could care less right now. "I'll have another one, please," I say to the bartender for about the tenth time.

"Long night?" he says with a smile as he pushes my gin and tonic towards me.

I scoff. "Yeah."

He leans against the bar, his dark hair flopping down just past his eyes. "We're almost closing here."

I narrow my eyes at him. "You speak good English."

He lets out a hardy laugh. "Only for people like you."

I don't know why it makes me all defensive and mad, but it does. "*Ma io sono italiano.*"

"I know. The whole world knows. I just mean that because my restaurant is on the main strip, a lot of English speaking tourists come around here."

I take another drink. "You must be really busy then."

He shrugs his shoulders. "Yeah, but tonight there was this small concert that took all of my customers away."

I lean against the bar, getting closer to his deep olive eyes. "Really?" I raise my eyebrows at him.

His lips turn up in a small smile. "Yes, it was some group called Insieme, I don't know if you've ever heard of them."

I put my hand to my chin and make a loud *hum* sound. "I think I heard their song on the radio the other day, actually. To be honest, they are *so* overrated."

He lets out that sweet laugh again and moves from behind the bar and sits next to me. "I totally wouldn't freak out if one of the members were to be one of my customers."

I take another sip, finishing my drink. "I'm sure they would be lovely to meet."

"Me too."

"May I get another drink?"

He cocks his head and makes his eyes big. "Your bill is piling up, *amore mia*."

A laugh escapes my lips, but without any emotion behind it. "My boyfriend always calls me that." My stomach drops at the reminder of Luca.

"Where is Luca?"

I shrug my shoulders. "He was tired."

I stormed off on him.

I'm still mad at Luca, though. Yes, I would give him a hard time about not going out with Tony and I, but he eventually came around. There have been several occasions where Luca was the one asking us to go out. It's not like I'm the only one to blame here.

But is there really anything to blame? I mean, Mary doesn't even *know* what it's like out here. She just sees the articles, which are fake half of the time. Yes, I haven't been calling her as often and I have been letting her calls go to voicemail, but it's not like I do it on purpose. I'm busy with concerts, and sometimes I don't want to pick up my phone. Is that such a crime? No, I don't think so.

I thought Luca and I had a trusting relationship, and Mary for that matter. I thought we told each other everything. Insieme doesn't keep secrets.

"If you don't mind, I'd like that drink." I smile.

He gets up and pours me another drink. "Do you need to talk?"

My smile fades and I set my lips into a firm line. I know I shouldn't, but it would be nice to get an unbiased opinion. "I love and hate being on tour."

He sits back next to me. "It can be difficult."

I love when people pretend like they understand what I'm going through. Hell, I don't even understand my own feelings, so how could anyone understand?

I finish my new drink in two sips. "I wouldn't change it for anything."

But maybe I could have done things differently. Maybe I didn't have to jump into this head first at 16. I wasn't prepared for all the eyes that would follow me. I wasn't prepared to be a role model to the whole world; I wasn't prepared for all the pressure.

I try to hide my tears that are starting to pool in my eyes, but of course, I fail miserably. "I'm just so exhausted with everyone being so concerned about me. Lately, it feels like my close friends have been judging me."

"What do you mean?"

I know I shouldn't be telling some stranger this; he could leak the information. But I'm too drunk to even care right now. My head is pounding with thoughts, ready to burst into three million pieces if I don't let it out soon.

"They think I'm going crazy."

"Are you?"

"No."

"So maybe it's time to tell them that you're fine."

I look at him and give him a warm smile. "I don't do well with confrontation."

"Sometimes it's better to have those tough conversations and let people know you're upset, rather than staying quiet and slowly drifting away from them without any explanation."

I stand up, my knees wobbling. I can't feel any limbs in my body, everything tingles. I chuckle a little. "How are you so good at giving advice?"

He walks me to the door and gives me two kisses on the cheek. I try not to push him off of me because I know he's just doing what he usually does due to his Italian culture, but I don't want another man touching me if it isn't Luca.

You can still love someone and be frustrated with them.

"Trust me, I deal with your kind on a daily basis."

Your kind?

I stumble into the hotel room. I'm a thousand degrees, I can feel my clothes sticking to my sweaty body, I can't control my breathing. I'm going to throw up.

I bolt for the bathroom at the same time that Luca emerges from his bedroom. I drop to my knees in front of the toilet and Luca is right by my side, holding back my hair.

"It's okay," he whispers over and over.

Once my stomach is empty and everything I've ever eaten or drank is now officially down the toilet drain, I look up at Luca. "I'm sorry I woke you up."

He's dressed in his white tank-top and baby blue shorts. Of course he has his gold chain on, making himself look like a cast member straight out of *GoodFellas*, making my heart skip a beat.

"Don't be sorry."

I purse my lips together. "We need to talk," I whisper. He nods and lifts me off the floor, carrying me like a newly wedded couple. He places me down gently on the couch and sits across from me on the chair. I wish I was wrapped up in his arms, I wish we weren't so far apart.

"What's up?" he asks.

I swallow down my nerves. I can sing in front of thousands of people no problem, but talking to Luca? Oh gosh, it's actually tragic how nervous I get around him.

"Why didn't you tell me Mary talked to you?"

He doesn't break eye contact, he looks like he expected that question. "I don't know."

I cross my legs and shake my head to the side, looking at the floor. "You obviously agree with her if you didn't tell me about it."

"Giovanna, I just held back your hair while you puked your guts out literally five seconds ago. Don't pretend like I don't have to keep an eye on you."

I shut my eyes. "Luca, please, it was a yes or no question."

He stands up. "You want to know the truth?"

I stand up, walking over to him. "I would love that."

"Fine. I think you're going crazy out here. I don't know what has gotten into you, but ever since we won the Grammy, you've been going nonstop. You're always drinking. You're always dancing. You're never writing songs anymore. You're always looking for the next best party and you don't give a damn about how your actions affect me or Tony. Partying has taken priority over Insieme."

I put my finger on his chest. "I am *so* sick and tired of you acting as if you aren't right by my side when we're at the club!"

"See!" he screams, veins popping out of his neck. "This is why I never open up to you about anything. You're so quick to get defensive; you never let me finish what I'm saying."

"Because you're acting as if I'm a child!"

He balls his hands into a frustrated fist and throws them down with rage. "Shut up for two damn minutes!" I shiver, shutting my mouth. "I love you, but how long can this last? We don't have a backup plan, so yes, I am concerned that you're treating singing like a hobby instead of your career."

I furrow my brows together, twisting my mouth with distaste. He's the one who made me dropout, I told him this was going to happen! "Oh, I know this is my career. This is all I fucking do now! When do we get a break? Do you see how overworked we are? We have to be up early everyday and workout, we have to record new songs on our tour bus now, we are constantly in and out of interviews, and we haven't been able to visit our family in a year. So don't you *dare* say that I'm not putting in the work."

He's shaking his head. "I get it."

"What the hell is up with everyone saying that to me?" I don't like how mean I'm being, but does he really get it? I thought he was the only person who could understand me. I thought he and Mary knew exactly what I was feeling without me having to say a word.

I was wrong.

"You clearly think I'm just wasting away my time," I continue. "You think that so much that you are keeping an eye on me now."

"I never said you aren't putting in the work," he says slowly.

"Good. I would hate for you to think that, especially since I write all the songs."

"What is going on?" Tony says, rubbing his eyes as he walks out of his bedroom.

I exhale loudly. "Luca and Mary are treating me like I'm some eight-year-old."

"STOP GIVING US A REASON TO," Luca yells.

"Hey!" Tony tries to get his attention, but it's a lost cause.

"This needs to stop, Gia. You're partying too much. Once in a while, maybe once a week, it would be acceptable. But do you really need to get wasted every night?"

Yes. I don't know how to explain it. Drinking makes me forget all of the deadlines; all the stress. I thought singing would be fun, I thought it would be a big fairytail. I didn't know how much work goes on behind the scenes. Sometimes a drink is the only thing that keeps me sane.

When I feel like not getting out of bed, I get up because I know that I'll go out at night. I need the alcohol in my system so I can fake a smile to the press. Do you know what it's like to have so many people watching you? So what do I do in order to care a little less about all the judgment? I drink.

"Okay," Tony whispers. "I don't have time for you guys to be arguing like a couple who has been married for thirty years."

I scoff, staring directly at Luca. "We're not married."

The conversation I had with Antonio when I was visiting rings in the back of my mind. Where do I see this relationship going? It's been five years and he *still* hasn't proposed. I don't want to give him an ultimatum because if he really wanted to, he would have by now.

"Gia," Luca says, "it's much more complicated than you think."

I open my arms and drop them to the side, my whole body deflating. "Then enlighten me, Luca." My voice cracks. "Please tell me why we've been together for so long and you say 'I love you' everyday, but yet you haven't asked the question."

He takes a seat, and this makes my heart go rampid. He grips his hair, clearly stressed and trying to find the right words.

"It's because you don't want to marry somebody you have to babysit, isn't it?" I offer, hoping that's not the answer. In the back of my mind, though, I know that's how he feels. He did this to me when I was dating Danny, he's doing it to me again. He explodes and then feels bad about it.

Wait, is he seriously crying right now? How is he the one crying when he just woke the whole hotel up when he was yelling at me?

"Gia," he says again.

"What is it, Luca?" I try to keep calm, but it's not working out very well for me.

"I can't propose to you." His voice is so weak, so unrecognizable. Here comes my tears.

"Why?" I sit next to him and put my hand gently on his knee. I never *want* to fight with Luca, despite our ups and downs. I don't have to always be right, we don't always have to see eye to eye, but I know that what he's about to say is clearly bothering him.

He shakes his head. "I don't know how to say it."

"You need to say it," Tony buds in. "She has the right to know."

Even Tony knows? "Tell me," I urge.

"Samantha won't let me," he mumbles.

"Huh?" I blurt. Maybe I misheard.

He looks up at me with tears in his pleading eyes. "Reen won't let me get married."

"Why?" I let out a shaky breath. "Why do they even care?"

He shuts his eyes. "I don't know."

"Well, what did they say?" I demand, coming off as if I'm mad at Luca, but I'm really just trying to understand the situation and he won't spit it out.

"They think it's a bad marketing move," Tony explains for Luca. "Luca has so many girls who are madly in love with him, and they think that if he gets married, it will drop our fanbase."

I make my eyes big, blinking several times. "How does that make any sense? Luca and I are publicly dating."

"I know, that's what I told them," Luca says. "They told me that... I can't even say it. It makes me sick."

"They basically said that fans still have this false hope that Luca somehow might magically fall in love with them. If he were to marry you, it would 'officially take him off the market' is what they said," Tony explains.

"But how did this conversation even get brought up?" I'm trying to suppress my anger. I don't want to do anything I will regret, but with every passing second, I just want to find Samantha. I want to punch each and every single member of my management.

"Well, you were late to the studio one day," Luca says sheepishly. "You were drinking the night before." It's still a sensitive topic we have to discuss, but we can figure that out later. "I had the ring in my jacket pocket, and Tony was digging in there because he was looking for my phone to call you. I completely forgot it was there when I told him to get my phone and get you down here; it was supposed to be a surprise.

"You know how Tony is, of course he made a big deal about it. It's not his fault though, he was just being my best friend and he was excited for me. He was talking loudly, and he opened the box to look at it."

He gets up and starts pacing now, rubbing his sweaty hands up and down his thigh.

"We didn't hear Samantha come into the studio, and by the time we saw her, she had already seen the ring. She put two and two together and then she sat me down and gave me the whole talk about why I couldn't purpose to you."

We're all crying uncontrollably, but I'm the worst one out of all three of them. "Oh," I say.

Luca drops to both knees in front of me, taking both of my hands in his. A perfect fit. Everything is right between us.

Except our management.

"Giovanna, I would never ask you to give all of this up," he urges. "But I'm asking you to give up the bars. I'm asking you to not be mad at me because I haven't put a ring on your finger, because believe me, I picked out the perfect ring for you. I love you, Giovanna. I am so sorry that this is happening to us."

My jaw tenses as I swallow. "I can't, Luca," I whisper. I can't stay in this toxic management environment without a drink to help me through it all. I can't do it on my own. "I can't give it up when it's all I have left."

Chapter 35

I STORM OUT OF our sweet and down the hallway before the boys can stop me. I bang my fist on her door, waking up the whole hotel in the process.

"Samantha!" I yell. I can hear her get out of bed as I keep pounding on her door.

"Do you have any idea what time it is?" she asks, rubbing the sleep out of her eyes.

I march into her room, slamming the door behind me. "No, do *you* have any idea how much you've hurt me?"

"What are you talking about?"

I get all up in her face to the point where I can see the tiny freckles on her cheeks. "Do you love him?" I lower my voice.

"Have you been drinking? What the hell are you talking about?" She lets me in and I don't bother to close the door behind me.

I ball my fists at my sides. Yes, I've been drinking, but what the hell does that have to do with anything right now?

"Just answer the question: are you in love with Luca? Is that why you won't let him marry me?" I choke on my tears.

"Oh."

"Yeah. Please explain to me. Explain to me the reasoning behind your need to control my life."

She puts her hands on me and guides me to the edge of her bed. I am fuming.

"Don't touch me," I whisper.

"Giovanna, let me explain."

"Please enlighten me," I snap.

And she does. For the next twenty minutes I just sit silently on her bed as she talks to me. She's never seen me like this; she must be scared of me. I'm like a ticking time bomb full of rage, ready to explode at any given moment and destroy anything and everything around me.

She says our fans will get bored with us, we'll go broke, and Insieme will all go to shit. I'm paraphrasing, of course, but that's basically it in a nutshell. Reen won't let me be Mrs. Fonzo. I always thought Giovanna Fonzo had a nice ring to it, but it doesn't matter what I think anymore. It never really mattered what I thought, I was just a pawn in this chess game.

"Now do you understand?" she asks without a hint of sympathy in her voice. She doesn't regret it. She doesn't care how much I'm hurting.

Will people ever stop hurting me? No. I don't think they will. I'm always disappointed.

I shake my head. "No. I don't understand. Don't you think fans will be happy for me?"

She gives a cold laugh. "Welcome to Hollywood, dear." I hate her tone. I hate how she's acting like this is normal. "You knew what you were signing up for when you chose this lifestyle."

I shake my head; that isn't the case at all. What is the point of it all?

"I can't believe you. I thought we were friends."

So many betrayals in such a short amount of time.

It's crazy how much your life can change in a matter of hours.

"There is not much I can do, unless you want to give all this up. Is that what you really want?"

I don't know.

I don't know.

I DON'T KNOW ANYMORE.

"I'll tell you right now that if you walk away from all of this over some *boy*, you will regret it for the rest of your life. I don't care how in love you think you are- how perfect you think he is- you will not give this up for him. You would be stupid to."

But I love him. He's the only person who's ever made me feel loved. He's the only person who made me feel okay being myself.

He loves me and my flaws.

"I know you love it all too much to walk away from this contract. You love the stage, the parties, the fame, the *glory*. You eat it all up and soak it all in, so don't lie to me and don't lie to yourself and pretend like you're seriously considering leaving Reen."

"Stop," I breathe.

"You may be mad at me right now, but I promise you that if you get married, your fanbase will drop tremendously."

"And how do you know that?" My questions are getting weaker and weaker. I'm getting tired of fighting.

"I've been in this industry long enough, I've seen this happen before with my own two eyes, you have to believe me, Giovanna."

"Don't pretend like you're doing this for my best interest," I spit out. "You selfish, pretentious little piece of-"

"Gia," Luca interrupts, barging through the door frame. He comes to my side, practically pushing Samantha out of his way. "Gia, it's okay, I'm right here." I accept his hug, putting all of my weight into him.

He picks me up and glares at Samantha over his shoulder before walking out of her room. I'm so upset, so frustrated, and so…

Defeated.

When he gets back to our sweet, he places me down on my bed and lays beside me. I curl into his arms like I usually do. I'm at home again. He strokes my shoulder gently; I didn't know anyone was capable of having so many tears in their system, but here I am.

"Luca?" I ask, unsure if he's awake or not because his breathing has gotten heavier and slower.

"Yes, *amore*."

I shut my eyes and press my body closer to his. "Please, just take all of the pain away. I can't handle it anymore."

Chapter 36

FOR THE REST OF the tour, I don't enjoy myself at all. I feel sick everytime I'm on stage. I feel repulsed just being in the same room as Samantha. Of course, Reen didn't budge, despite how many times I yelled. It was like a screaming twenty-three-year-old was completely normal to them; they were unfazed.

So after about two months, I just stopped everything.

I stopped yelling, I stopped asking questions, I stopped pleading my case, and I stopped writing songs. But I went back to my family, but they would describe me as a shell; lifeless and only going through motions instead of enjoying them.

I went numb.

I'm tired of trying to be perfect in order to be accepted. I am tired of everything.

But at least I have Luca, right? At least I have Insieme, Tony, and my family, right?

Except I feel completely empty and alone in a room full of friends and family.

My parents don't know about the engagement situation, because why would I bother them with my problems? I'm the strong one. I'm the one who is going to light the world on fire. I have my shit together. According to them, I'm bound to rule the world. But they can sense something is off, everyone can.

Yet I am successful, and I've never felt more alone.

What is the point of being in a relationship if we can't get married? But what's the point in staying with Reen if they don't let me be free? I understand that they are my boss, but I still have the right to make my own decisions, don't I?

I don't know anymore.

I have no answers.

I have no thoughts. No feelings.

Numb.

To be honest, I've never felt farther apart from the boys than we are right now. Insieme is anything but together. They are concerned about me. They say that I'm "acting out", but what else am I supposed to do?

They've stopped going to the clubs and bars with me, and it's to the point that they don't even ask if I'm going out because they already know where I'm headed off to.

I can see that Luca wants to say something, but I also see him bite his tongue down every night. I see Tony exchange glances with him, the two of them having a silent conversation about me.

I don't expect them to understand how I'm acting.

I didn't know one could just simply stop feeling.

"Want another one?" The bartender asks.

I barely nod and he pours another drink for me. "Thank you," I whisper. Tears fill my eyes as I think about how I ended up at this bar.

I was so excited to go to Europe, but I didn't enjoy my time at all. It feels like I'm a hamster running on a wheel, getting no further ahead or behind, all while looking directly in front of me.

Now that I'm back in Los Angeles, I actually realize how comfortable I've made myself here. It feels like home, at least I have that.

My phone buzzes in my pocket and I reach for it as I take another sip from my drink. I roll my eyes at the headline of another article. If one more person takes a picture of me at the bar, I'm going to punch somebody.

Seriously? They act as if I'm committing a crime just by having a few drinks. Maybe I don't want to get all dressed up in my mini dresses and high heels and my gold hoops, but that doesn't mean I'm going through a "midlife crisis". It just means I'm a regular person who wants to wear sweatpants and have a drink on this fine Tuesday evening.

"Is everything alright?" the bartender asks.

"Yep," I say coldly. I've learned not to talk to anyone, it's a waste of time. People love to pretend like they care, but they really, really don't.

My phone starts ringing and Luca's name appears across my screen. "Yeah," I say.

"Gia, where the hell are you?"

"I don't know." I just walk into the nearest bar I can find, I genuinely don't know where I am.

"Get home right now, Samantha is here."

I stand up, nearly falling over, but I'm able to handle my alcohol a lot better now. "What's going on? Is she there to tell me that we can get married?" It sounds like I'm mad at him, but he knows that I'm just frustrated that I literally have no control over my own life.

"Get here right now, Gia, I'm serious."

"I'll be there in two minutes," I say, trying to hide my emotions, but I'm shitting my pants. Luca doesn't get annoyed easily, and lately he's been making jokes about marrying me to make light of the situation, and usually I'm the one being short with him because he's turned into a little asshole.

Something must be wrong. I drop cash on the bar and dash out of there, get into a taxi and go tumbling through my front door.

Samantha is standing in front of the boys with her arms folded, and the boys are sitting on the couch. Every pair of eyes in the room lands on me, and I feel self conscious. I don't feel like they're judging me, I *know* they're judging me by the look in their eyes.

"Sit down," Samantha demands, sounding as cold as ever. To say our friendship has been strained lately would be an understatement, so her behavior isn't concerning to me. What's concerning me is that the boys are radiating anger, and neither one of them are looking at me anymore.

"What happened?" I ask.

"Giovanna, what day is it today?" Samantha asks, starting to pace back and forth.

"I don't know." My days have started to mesh together in a big heep. I wake up, throw up, I'm forced to workout, then I go to the occasional concert, go to a bar, and then stumble my way back to bed. How am I supposed to know what day it is?

Tony scoffs. "Of course you don't know."

"What is that supposed to mean?" I snap. I'm not a laughing, happy drunk anymore. I've turned into a mean drunk. "Does somebody want to explain what the hell is going on?"

"I'll tell you what's going on," Samantha says. "But just go ahead and look at the date on that fancy Apple Watch you bought yourself."

I check my watch and squint, trying to focus my eyes. "June 13," I say.

So..?

Luca drops his head and shakes it, disappointment swarming him. "You told us you had songs."

"June 13," I repeat, slowly this time. June 13, June 13, June 13, what's so special about today? Maybe I forgot to wish Samantha a happy birthday? Am I forgetting something?

"How could you do this to us?" Luca asks, looking at me with tears in his eyes.

Shit. Shit. Shit.

June 13.

My eyes go wide with realization. "I just need one more day." I don't know how I end up on my knees, especially in front of Samantha, but I do. "I'm begging you for just one more day."

"We thought you were writing songs, especially with all the time you've been spending getting experience," Luca says bitterly. "How the hell could you have *nothing*? Even Tony and I have come up with musical parts just in case you gave us lyrics."

"The due date just kind of snuck up on me," I explain, but even I don't understand my reasoning.

How could I forget the day that the album was due?

"So many fans are disappointed," Samantha states the obvious, as if I didn't already know that. "This doesn't look good for you."

"Okay, but why didn't you guys say anything to me?" I look at the boys. "You guys didn't think to remind me?"

"How could you forget about this?" Tony asks, rising to his feet. "I get that you're dealing with a lot of shit, but we signed the same contract too. Suck it the fuck up. You're ruining this for everyone."

"Do you know how many times we tried to call you and you just let us go to voicemail?" Luca asks, standing up too. "Do you know how many times I told you to stop drinking and you just yelled at me? You told me to stop babysitting you, so that's exactly what I did. I gave you space. I mean, am I even in a relationship anymore? You don't come home until four in the morning, you don't tell me you love you, you don't put any effort into anything, and now you're putting *my* career at risk." His voice could break the windows right now, I'm surprised they haven't shattered into a million pieces like my heart has in my chest. "Vince was right," he spits.

How many times can my little heart be broken?

"You fucked up big time," he continues. "Don't." He stops me when I open my mouth.

"Don't even. You can't explain this, you can't justify this."

"I'm sorry," I say. "I just need one more day and I'll have your album for you."

Samantha shakes her head. "You're a loose cannon, Giovanna. We don't know where you are, we don't know what you're saying to the press, all we know is that you're drinking yourself to death."

"I'm surprised your liver is still functioning," Tony sneers, looking me up and down. Full of so much rage, full of so much disappointment.

"I don't know what to say."

"Don't you start crying now," Luca says. "You brought this on yourself. You lost the deal."

I lost what now?

"What?" I ask breathlessly.

"Reen can no longer put up with your bullshit," Tony says.

"We've had to cover up for you in the media multiple times, but we just can't control you."

"That's so ironic," I say, wanting to punch Samantha in the face.

"We promised the fans a release date, and now Insieme won't be able to meet that deadline because you didn't turn anything in," she continues, ignoring me. "You are spending money before you even get it. You are blowing through more booze than I even thought was imaginable. You are too much of a liability," Samantha lists off bad thing after bad thing. "Reen is cutting ties with Insieme."

What?

No.

I must be dreaming. I can wake up now.

"You're joking," I laugh. "There's no fucking way you're letting go of us."

They can't do that. What happened to the contract? So when it comes to marriage, I have to listen to my contract, but when I'm one day late for a couple of songs, they are dropping us?

"She's serious." Luca can't stop shaking.

"I will be back tomorrow morning to get all the paperwork sorted out, but until then, try not to get yourself killed, lay off the drinks a little bit," Samantha comments before walking out the door.

"I'm so sorry-"

"Save it," Tony interrupts. "You've done enough."

If I still had a whole heart, I would say that Samantha put a knife in it and the boys are now twisting it until I bleed out.

But how can you stab a broken heart?

This doesn't feel real. "I'm sure we can figure something out."

Luca pulls at his hair. "Giovanna, shut up. Please, just shut the hell up. You can't keep doing this. You can't be so selfish and act surprised when people get tired of your shit and leave you."

Not Luca. Please, anything but Luca.

"I should have never left everything behind for a girl like you!" he screams. "What was I thinking? Since when do I put an alcoholic over my own brother?"

"Luca, stop," I pleaded.

"You lost our record deal," Luca continues. "You only care about yourself. Giovanna, we're done."

"You're breaking up with me?" I ask, defeated.

His silence is enough of an answer for me.

"You told us you had a couple of ideas," Tony says. "When we asked you to see the album, you said to wait because it wasn't perfect."

Luca and I are done. I can't think straight, I can't stand. I sit down on the hardwood floor. This is all so much, all because I can't get my shit together.

I can't even be mad at the boys, it's all my fault.

"You're right," I say, looking up at them. I stand up and head for the door. "Yeah, I messed up." At least I can admit it. "But you know what? Did you ever stop to think that maybe I was crying out for help?"

Luca slams his hand down on the coffee table, causing me to pause mid stride. "You don't get to manipulate us this time! Enough, Giovanna! You lost the deal. *You.* We have nothing now because of *you.* I don't care how exhausted you are, you could have always talked to us. We always made sure we were there for you, and you just spat in our face and wasted five years of our life."

"No, don't say that," I fire back. "I know you're upset with me, but don't you *dare* say that the past five years have been a waste of time."

He throws his hands up. "If you loved us- if you *truly* loved us- you wouldn't have ruined our lives. You are so selfish. How could you do this to us?"

"Now we have to go move back to our families because we have no purpose in being here anymore," Tony says. "Let me make one thing clear: once all the paperwork is cleared up and we've cut all ties with you, don't call us. Don't even think about us. You made your bed, you can lie in it. I'm done defending you, Giovanna."

How am I losing everything and everyone? How did I get to this point?

"Point taken," I whisper.

A few months ago, I was on top of the world. I was unstoppable and Insieme was at the peak of our fame. Everyone knew who we were, everyone wanted to be us.

I took it for granted.

I thought I hit rock bottom when I found out I couldn't get married to the love of my life, but I was wrong. If there's one thing I've learned from the last five years, it's this: just when you think you've hit rock bottom, there's always a farther way to go.

I had it all, now I have nothing.

I'm not some kid with a dream, I'm a grown adult who has single handedly destroyed the lives of two of my closest friends.

I lost everyone and everything. Mary. Tony. Luca. My family and I aren't as close. The fame. Insieme. My will to be the best version of myself.

I hate myself for losing it all. I don't think I'll ever be able to forgive myself, so I don't expect the boys to forgive me.

So I do the only thing left for me to do, I leave. I walk out of the door, I walk away from the boys. I walk away from the life I learned and grew to love.

I sit down on the driveway and throw my head between my knees, crying out so loud.

It's all my fault.

I lost the only good thing that has ever happened in my life.

I am lost.

And I don't think I can bounce back this time.

I have no one.

So I sit there, the only noise that fills the air is the sound of my muffled tears.

I am alone. I am at my lowest, without my family around me.

If I knew life on the road would be this difficult, I would have just taken that stupid dream to my grave.

Acknowledgements

I would first and foremost like to thank my family. To my parents, who continue to push me to be the best version of myself. To my brother, who has always and will always be my best friend.

I would also like to thank my cover designer, Isabella Alvarez Lalama for the beautiful cover. You made my vision come to life and had to work with my terrible communication skills, so thank you.

To the fans, it is crazy to see all the love you have given to me, and I am forever grateful for it. Thank you for supporting me every step of the way.

And finally, to my extended family and friends, thank you for continually asking me about my book. This one was for you.